I kicked open the white wooden door and brought Wilhelmina out from under my jacket as I entered the room. The blinding, white sunlight streamed into the cabana and illuminated Nozdrev.

"If you want to live," I said, "don't move." I waved the luger as he moved his hand toward his chest. His hand retreated. Again he lifted his hand toward his chest, but he didn't complete the gesture.

Then I noticed the spot of red near the shoulder of his white beachrobe, and the slowly-forming pool of red on the white tile floor of the cabana . . .

NICK CARTER IS IT!

NC-A

From The Nick Carter Killmaster Series

Dedicated to the Men of the Secret
Services of the United States of
America.

A Killmaster Spy Chiller

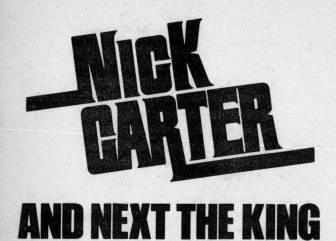

NICK CARTER

AND NEXT THE KING

CHARTER
NEW YORK

A DIVISION OF CHARTER COMMUNICATIONS INC.
A GROSSET & DUNLAP COMPANY

AND NEXT THE KING

Charter Books
A division of Charter Communications Inc.
A Grosset & Dunlap Company
360 Park Avenue South
New York, New York 10010

First Charter edition published May 1980

2 4 6 8 0 9 7 5 3 1
Manufactured in the United States of America

AND NEXT THE KING

Chapter One

The midday California sun sent glimmers off the deep blue water. Her pale blond hair was like a diamond against the blue, as she swam across the Olympic-sized pool.

Her house was named "Paradise," and paradise it was: a long, white luxurious structure set among the pool and citrus gardens and beautifully manicured lawns. High in the hills above Los Angeles it had the most spectacular view of the city you could imagine. Even the smog seemed to have taken its leave up here, at least temporarily.

I'd flown out here for a much needed R and R after a brutal job in Athens. She had met me at the airport and immediately spirited me up to this haven. She'd cancelled all of her appointments, and for a week now it had been just the two of us. Even her servants kept discreetly out of sight. During the day we explored the nearby hills and swam and lay beside the pool. At night we watched the stars from her glass-enclosed living room and then lay for hours on the satin sheets of her large oval bed. We satisfied our desires until both of us were exhausted and then drifted into sleep, usually not until near dawn. Paradise it certainly was.

She finished her lap, and as though she sensed my presence, she looked toward the terrace where I stood. She saw me and her sensuous lips parted in a smile over those perfect white teeth.

"Come on in, the water's fine," she called. That was no surprise; the water was always fine here.

"Come on in," she repeated in that sophisticated, sultry voice, which was a delightful contrast to the perfect innocence of her face. It's a voice you'd recognize. And you'd recognize the face too. Her name is Susan and for the last couple of years she's been one of the top actresses in pictures, a genuine star.

I liked watching her glide across the pool, but I knew I'd like being in the pool even more. I shucked my clothes, walked down the half dozen flagstone steps from the terrace to the pool, and dived in. I opened my eyes under water and swam toward those long shapely legs, now treading water with all the grace of a ballet dancer. I reached out and encircled her legs with my arms and then moved my hand up to her tanned, undulating stomach. Slowly she slid underwater, her legs, her torso, her full breasts gliding past my eyes. And then her face was opposite mine. Our bodies moved together underwater, and I felt an electric shock as her breasts moved against my chest; and I felt her quiver too. I moved my tongue to her mouth and taking her in my arms, floated us both to the bottom of the pool. We lay there in a passionate embrace, like two sea creatures, lost in time. Finally she moved her hand against my cheek, indicating that she needed air. I held her firmly and sprung us both to the surface of the water. I placed my right arm around her rib cage, cupping one of her beautiful breasts in my hand. With my other arm I sidestroked to the edge of the pool, carrying her beside me.

"Here, darling," she said, almost breathlessly, as we reached the blue-tiled side of the pool.

She stretched out her arms to brace herself and then flattened her backside against the tiles. I entered her in a single thrust, displacing the water between us. Our bodies moved like one, sending ripples back across the pool's entire surface. The ripples became waves as our own intensity increased. As we reached a peak, she cried out like a creature from the nearby hills.

Afterwards we lay on the warm flagstones of the terrace. Her eyes were closed against the sun, and I traced a remaining rivulet of water down her fine, firm breasts. The sun seemed to give energy to my own drained body, and lying there beside her I felt more peaceful than I'd felt in a long, long while. I stretched back and watched a bank of cumulus clouds move against the blue sky. The only sounds were of a blackbird chirping in the nearby woods and of a telephone ringing in the distance.

"Telephone for Mr. Brody," the maid's voice announced over the intercom system.

That was me. Brody, Charles Brody, was the name Susan knew me by. She smiled up at me as I lifted my body from the ground, but I wasn't smiling. Only one person had my phone number here. And a call from him could only mean one thing.

I moved to a phone which sat on a glass table near us.

"Hello."

"Mr. Carter?" It was a no-nonsense man's voice.

"Yes."

"David Hawk wants you to fly to Washington and meet with him immediately. He says it's top priority. Urgent."

I looked at the golden vision of Susan lying below me and couldn't help sighing inwardly. But Hawk was my boss and when he said go, I went. That was the way it was. Scratch the remaining two weeks of my R and R.

"Will there be a plane for me?"

"There's one waiting for you now at the Hollywood-Burbank Airport," the man said and hung up.

I replaced the receiver and reached for a towel.

"What is it?" Susan asked.

"I have to leave immediately."

She stood up and moved toward me like the goddess that she was.

"No, darling." Her face formed itself into a pout.

"Yes."

"But why?" The pout was changing to a look that meant she was coming close to tears.

"My law firm has business that only I can handle. I have to go overseas, I expect. Sorry, love."

She blinked back a tear and then smiled her dazzling smile. She wasn't an actress for nothing.

"Sometimes, you know, I really think you're a spy or something the way you're always running off," she said, attempting to make the best of a bad situation by joking.

"Well," I joked back, "I think you shouldn't

start believing those movies you're in."

She laughed. "No, I suppose not," she said, and moved her body next to mine. I bent down and kissed her and then turned to put on my clothes. There was no time for a long goodbye.

"A spy or something," Susan had joked, except it wasn't a joke, and my work went way beyond the kind of tame spy stuff you usually see in the movies. Killmaster N3 was my AXE designation. AXE did the jobs the other agencies couldn't handle, and I hadn't earned my rank just by stealing an occasional secret or protecting visiting dignitaries.

As I navigated a Jaguar down the narrow, hilly road from Susan's house, I couldn't help wondering why Hawk needed me. There were a number of AXE agents who could do *just about* any job that came up. When I'd returned from Greece, it had been Hawk's idea for me to take a break. His parting words had been, "See you in three weeks, Nick. Unless," he'd added sardonically, "a major international crisis comes up." So it looked like I was heading straight into a major international crisis.

As there weren't many houses up this far, the road I was traveling on toward the freeway was pretty much deserted. But as I turned a curve I noticed two motorcycles sitting on a side road. As I passed they turned onto the road and soon they were right up behind me, too close for comfort on a road full of sharp turns and dramatically steep descents. I caught them in my rearview mirror: two dirty-looking bikers on big choppers. One was a big man with shoulder-length, greasy-looking hair, his buddy a smaller man who'd gone in the opposite direction in his hairdo: his head was shaved completely bald. The bald man was bare-chested. The other one wore a black leather vest. And they both had swastikas hanging on their gleaming torsos.

When they pulled their choppers right up beside me, I began to get really uncomfortable. What the hell were they doing? On a road this narrow and blind, if another car appeared ahead there was either going to be a crash or someone would go hurtling over the side of the hill.

"Hey, man!" the bigger biker yelled at me, "Pull over! Stop!"

"Why?" I yelled back and kept up my speed.

"You're taking up too much road, man, that's why. We wanna talk to you." I realized then that these punks were out for what they considered some kicks. But even if I'd liked their kind of kicks —which I didn't—I didn't have time for them. Not with a plane waiting at the airport for me.

"Go to hell," I yelled back. The big one answered this by spitting in my direction. His gob didn't land in my face, but not for want of trying. It was just that his aim had been bad.

Then the big guy nodded to his buddy, and before I knew what was happening the bald guy pulled his chopper directly in front of the Jaguar. I had to slow down to avoid hitting him immediately. One bike was now at my side, the other in front of me, and to my other side was a drop of hundreds of feet into canyons that already had plenty of totalled cars and dead bodies. So this was their game: The motorcycle in front of me was slowing down, and the idea was that I would be forced to do the same and eventually stop.

But I was having none of it. I moved my foot from the brake to the accelerator and speeded up, nosing the front of the Jaguar into the back of the cycle before me. The bald guy didn't expect this and even if he had expected it, there wouldn't have been much he could do about it. He abruptly swerved his bike to the left to get away from me, but as he did so he nearly crashed into his buddy, who was still heading up my left. The bald guy gunned his engine to get away from his buddy and they missed each other by a fraction of an inch. But the sharp turn and the extra speed had sent the bald guy's bike into a tailspin. The bike abruptly crashed to the ground and sent its rider sprawling head first onto the road.

Unfortunately his friend was still beside me.

"You shouldn't have done that," he snarled. A few seconds later I saw a knife sail past my head and land in the leather of the passenger seat. I needed a knife there even less than I needed a gob of spit. I pulled the knife out of the leather with my right hand, steering with my left. These clowns had picked the wrong man to hassle with. I'd been trained to kill, with knives as well as with guns and explosives, and it would have been easy for me to toss the knife right into the bastard's head or his heart. But I kill only when I have to, on the job, not for personal reasons.

I aimed the knife carefully. The biker laughed when he saw me throw the knife, obviously thinking I was aiming at him and aiming badly. But his laugh disappeared in a second when the knife hit exactly where I'd intended: in his back tire. His face opened in an "O" of surprise as he lost control of the bike when the tire blew out from under him.

Now I did slow down to watch him careen wildly down the hill ahead of me before finally crashing into a patch of shrubs on the left side of the road. As I drove on I heard him shout. So he wasn't dead, just out of commission for awhile.

Then, through the rearview mirror, I saw that the bald guy had remounted his bike and was trying to catch up with me again. I reached under the seat and pulled out a long, thick piece of rope, and shaped it with my right hand into a cattleman's knot. I deliberately slacked my speed until the biker was beside me—right where I wanted him. His bald head had a long, bloody cut across its top and his nose and mouth were also a bloody pulp.

"I'll kill you," he yelled.

I didn't want to kill him, just get him out of my way and maybe put a dent in his overblown macho pride. I waited until we were heading toward a very sharp curve. Then suddenly I threw the rope and braked my car abruptly. The rope flew around his arms, pulling them from his handlebars and pinioning them to his chest. His bike went hurtling out from under him and sailed right over the edge of the cliff. He hit the ground in the middle of the road with a heavy thud. I heard his bike crash below. I let the rope slip out of my hand and drove ahead, leaving him struggling to untangle himself from the rope and cursing at me for destroying what was dearest to him: his bike. And I took off for the freeway.

Hawk had a Lear jet waiting for me at Hollywood-Burbank, and when I landed, six hours later, at Dulles International in D.C., Hawk him-

self was there to greet me. Only minutes after the
plane's wheels touched the ground, Hawk walked
into the jet's cabin. He had a scowl on his face and
one of his half-chewed, foul-smelling cigars in his
mouth. He indicated with a flick of his hand that I
was to stay seated and he moved to take the chair
opposite me.

"Been reading the papers, Nick," he asked, "or
been too preoccupied with the ladies?" A slight
smile flickered across his face.

"Well, sir, I did catch a couple of papers in
L.A."

"So you've read about the latest kidnapping in
Spain?"

I had. The day before, a high Spanish military
official, General Rodriguez, had been abducted by
a band of revolutionary terrorists who called themselves "El Grupo Febrero." From what I'd read,
they were a pretty vicious lot. Within the last two
months, they'd already killed the Spanish Minister
of the Treasury, the Minister of Education, two de-
puties of the Spanish Parliament, and a Special En-
voy of the King. In addition, they'd shot at and
crippled several other high government officials.
And they claimed responsibility for the bombing of
a government building that had killed twenty
more.

"A bad business," Hawk said.

"Yes, sir. Any ransom demand?"

"No, and I don't think there's going to be, Nick.
Hasn't ever been one. They're out for blood. They
kidnap these men, hold revolutionary 'trials,' then
torture them to death. It seems to me, and the
group has said as much in their communiqués, that

they're out to eliminate the entire Spanish government. Or as much of it as they can. And in the process, of course, they've got the whole country paralyzed."

It was, as Hawk said, a bad business. But from what he'd told me so far, I didn't see why Hawk needed me. Any of a dozen other AXE agents—to say nothing of the CIA—should have been able to track down General Rodriguez's abductors.

As though he'd read my thoughts, Hawk said, "The Spanish government requested our top man, Nick. You see, as bad as these other murders and kidnappings were, this one is much, much worse, more serious. It's not just another individual's death that's involved here. General Rodriguez was carrying important military secrets when they kidnapped him, secrets vital to the defense of Spain. They involve not just Spain's army and airforce, but," and here Hawk paused, "also the development of Spain's nuclear defense. You know what that means, Nick."

I knew what it meant, and it sent chills up and down my spine.

"What we're really afraid of, Nick, is that this Spanish group is part of some larger international terrorist organization, or that they at least have ties with other terrorist groups. When they find out that what they have in their hands is a plan for a nuclear weapon, who knows what's going to happen. This is just what I've been warning Washington about for years, with this spread of nuclear weapons: the possibility of them getting into the hands of a group of terrorists. I don't need to tell you, Nick, what kind of blackmail they can pull if they discover what they have. They'll have not just Spain in their paws, but the whole bloody world."

"Yes, sir."

"So, Nick, find those plans. And, if possible, save General Rodriguez's life."

"I'll try."

"Don't try. Do it. Now goodbye, Nick, and good luck."

"Am I to catch another plane here, sir?"

"No, stay on this one. It's been refueling while we talked. I didn't want to waste any time." Hawk turned and walked toward the door. Then at the doorway, he turned around and said, "And, Nick, don't forget the Russians." Then he left.

No, I wouldn't forget the Russians. And as I flew over the Atlantic I couldn't help thinking of what would happen if the Russians found out about the nuclear plan and reached the terrorists before I did. Of course, even the Russians would never supply nuclear weapons to a terrorist organization, but once the KGB found out the terrorists already had the plan, it was a safe bet that they'd want to play ball with them. And I had to find that plan before they started playing ball.

Chapter Two

Hawk had taken the precaution of registering the Lear to Milhautt, Lowry, and Bryan Associates, a New York City architectural firm. When I went through customs the passport I gave the official listed my name as David Bryan, my occupation as architectural engineer. I filled in "business," under *Purpose of Visit* and "two weeks" under *Length of Stay* on the form the official gave me. I just hoped, for the sake of Spain, and for my own sake, that my length of stay would be considerably less than two weeks.

I took a taxi at the airport to a small, quiet hotel, just a couple of blocks from the Prado. After checking in, I walked the ten blocks to the address Hawk had given me. I entered a large, modern office building and took the elevator to the tenth floor. Here I found the right suite and entered what looked like a typical modern office: beige carpet, beige walls, low-key, comfortable furniture, a suitably attractive secretary. This was the Spanish Intelligence Secret Forces Mission, and I was here to meet Ramon Lorca, Hawk's Spanish counterpart.

The secretary sat behind a desk near a door leading into an inner office and she was reading a fashion magazine when I entered. She looked up from her magazine and smiled. She was a pretty woman, around thirty, with large almond-shaped eyes and very white teeth.

"May I help you?" Her smile was dazzling.

"David Bryan. I believe I have an appointment."

"Ah, yes, Mr. Bryan," she inflected the name with a slight touch of irony as though she knew what my real name was. "Mr. Lorca has been expecting you." She picked up the phone and announced me to Mr. Lorca.

"Go right in," she said and motioned me toward the wood-paneled door leading into the inner office. She opened the door with a button concealed somewhere under her desk, and as the door swung open, I realized that the wood panels overlay a thick, bullet-proof sheet of metal, and that this wasn't, of course, the typical office it looked to be.

As the heavy door closed behind me, I found myself standing in a square office, with a floor-length expanse of glass windows along one of its sides. You could bet these windows were bullet-proof too. These windows let in so much light that at first I could only make out a dim figure rising from a desk in front of the windows and moving toward me. My eyes adjusted and I saw Ramon Lorca clearly as he took my hand, pumping it with a firm handshake.

"Welcome, Nick Carter," he said, in a deep, seasoned voice. "We are honored to have you among us." His greeting had no hint of flattery and his smile was friendly and sincere. He was a very large man, about my height. Beneath his elegantly cut white suit, his shoulders and arms were massive, like those of an ex-prizefighter, which he may well have been. His deeply tanned face had a classical Spanish profile, with his jet-black hair combed straight back. And his large, dark eyes were full of warmth. I knew right off that we were going to get along just fine.

"I thank you for coming, Mr. Carter. Your reputation, of course, precedes you," he said as he ushered me to a chair near his desk. I noticed that the glass windows looked out over the entire south of the city and that one could see the ochre-colored plains in the distance.

"I assume Hawk has explained to you what has happened, Mr. Carter."

"Yes."

"Well, frankly, Mr. Carter, we have almost no leads on the recent kidnapping or on any of the other kidnappings and assassinations. We need you, Mr. Carter. I regret to say I don't have any agents of your calibre on my staff. Except, if I may be so immodest, myself. But, as you see, they have me running the whole division now, and I don't get the chance to spend much time in the field anymore. Too many other priorities."

I should have guessed Lorca had been an agent himself. And a damn good one, I'd bet.

"Perhaps you should examine these first," he said, handing me a manilla file folder from his desk. "The men who were killed." The folder contained color morgue photographs of the officials who had been killed by El Grupo Febrero. I've seen some gory sights and plenty of dead men, but

I'd seldom seen a more gruesome example of cruelty than what El Grupo Febrero had done to these men. From the photographs you could see that all of them had been severely tortured before they'd been killed: Two men's genitals had been cut off, nearly all were missing fingernails. The singed body hair and the thin red lines on many of the men indicated that they'd been subjected to electric shock. Nearly all had large welts where they'd been beaten. And one man had all four of his limbs broken; he'd obviously been subjected to the rack.

I looked into Lorca's eyes, which were now hard and steely. "A vicious group," he said. "And the men they let live, the ones they shot down, it has been the same story. One man was shot deliberately in the genitals, another crippled in both legs, a third shot in the spine so that he is now paralyzed from the neck down."

Lorca said that he had no clues to the location of the group. They seemed to be operating all over Spain. The bombing of the government office had taken place in Madrid, as had all of the original kidnappings. But the bodies of the officials had been found all over Spain: one in Toledo, two in Barcelona, one in Granada, another in Seville. All the bodies had been found, at dawn, in town squares or public plazas. "They are deliberately making a mockery of the Spanish police," Lorca commented.

"We have connected El Grupo Febrero," Lorca continued, "to a group of dissidents of ten years ago. Strangely most of them were workers and college students, and at that time they do not seem to have been engaged in violence."

"The members of this organization?" I asked.

"That, I regret to say, is our main problem. You see, Mr. Carter, when the new government came into power, several years ago, the police and army had many, many files on the dissident groups. We had the names of members, detailed information about these men and women. But the new government decided that all of these files should be destroyed, except of course, for the obviously subversive groups, which, at the time, excluded El Grupo Febrero. I must admit to you that I approved of, even advocated, the destruction of these files. There were thousands and thousands of citizens listed as enemies of the state who were really only enemies of the former regime, so it seemed not only pointless but out of place in a democracy to retain all these files. In the case of El Grupo Febrero, however, I'm afraid we made a fatal mistake."

At this point Lorca was interrupted by a loud buzz from one of the telephones on his desk.

"That will be the police. I'm monitoring all of the calls that come into the police station, and when they receive one regarding this case, I have it transmitted up here so that I can listen." Lorca pushed a button beside one of the phones and we immediately heard the voices of a policeman and a young woman.

"Your name please?"

"I'm sorry, I can't give you that." Her voice was soft and very low. She was speaking almost in a whisper.

"But you have information on El Grupo Febrero?"

"I'm not sure." Her voice grew even softer. "I do think I should talk to someone."

"Can you come to the police station today?"

"No, I can't do that," she said, her voice rising, becoming almost shrill. She sounded frightened now. Lorca pressed another button, which was apparently a signal to the police station. For then the officer asked the woman to hold the line while he switched her to someone who might better be able to help her.

"I don't know . . ." she trailed off, and I was afraid she was going to hang up.

"Take the call, Nick," Lorca said. "You're in charge of this now, so you might as well start."

I picked up the phone Lorca indicated and spoke into it in my Castilian accent. I knew it wouldn't do any good to try to get the woman's name out of her; she was obviously too frightened to reveal that. But frightened of what? Of us? Of El Grupo Febrero? But I knew I had to keep her on the line (Lorca's men were no doubt tracing the call now) and I had to arrange to see her if I could. After identifying myself as a special agent working on the case, I decided to appeal to her emotions. Her soft voice indicated that she probably had some passionate ones.

"Miss, please, almost thirty people have already been killed. I've just been looking at the photographs of the men who have been tortured. El Grupo Febrero has promised to do this to many more. Please help us stop them before they can get to anyone else. *Any* information that you think might be connected with the group will help us."

There was a long pause. I almost thought that

she'd hung up. Then she said, "All right," very, very softly.

"I can't come to the police station," she said.

"Can I come to you?"

There was another very long pause.

"Will you be alone?" she finally asked.

"Yes."

"Two thirty-five Arboles," she said, "tonight after ten." Then she rang off immediately.

Lorca's face was grim when I hung up, and I expect mine was the same. It was a risky business, meeting her alone. It could be a trap, but it was a chance I had to take. Right now it was the only lead we had.

Another phone rang and Lorca picked it up. I watched him as he nodded into the phone, his fine Spanish profile troubled. When he hung up the phone, he turned to me.

"Three things," he said. "The woman's call was made in a phone booth near the Palace of Justice. My men weren't able to get there soon enough to see her, she wasn't on the phone long enough. Two, the house at two-three-five Arboles is listed in the name of one Pedro Salas, about whom we have nothing in the files. Three, the newspapers have just received another communique from El Grupo Febrero, saying that the nation can expect the trial to end by Friday, and that on Saturday they will strike again, this time, quote, 'as high as we can go.' "

Today was Monday.

"I guess I should check out General Rodriguez's office," I said.

"I thought you'd want to do that. I've already

sent word to the Defense Ministry that you'd be there sometime this afternoon. One final thing, Nick. I'll be frank with you. If this doesn't end soon, it's going to be catastrophic for my country. Unlike your country, Spain is a new and fragile democracy. It cannot stand the strain. Already there is talk of moving back to the days of Franco. I, personally, don't want that to happen, but we have to catch this group soon or the whole edifice will come tumbling down."

This strong man suddenly seemed very sad, not just for the killings, but for the fate of his nation. I wanted very much to help him.

I caught a taxi outside Lorca's office. As we drove through Madrid, I noticed that the streets were very deserted for this time of day in midweek. Then I remembered that it was siesta time, and that many people were now inside napping, avoiding the blazing afternoon sun. In a few hours they'd be back out to open their shops and socialize in the bars and cafes.

The Ministry of Defense was located in the huge complex of government buildings near the center of the city. Like the rest, it was an enormous, imperial-looking structure of white marble. Standing before it, at the top of a steep series of marble steps, were almost two dozen guards in full-dress military uniforms. I wondered if they were always there, or if they were on special duty as a result of the threats of El Grupo Febrero. A couple of the guards stood in front of me at the top of the steps, but I flashed the card Lorca had given me and sped past them into the building. Here I was stopped by another guard. I told him I was here to see General Pena, who was General Rodriguez's top aide. The guard steered me to the elevator where I met another guard. He telephoned up to General Pena's office before he let me enter the elevator. When I arrived on the fourth floor, I was met by still another guard. Security was tight here all right. The government seemed to be running scared. And for good reason.

I was escorted into General Pena's office, then the guard clicked his heels and exited, leaving me alone. General Pena's office could not have been more of a contrast to the one I'd just left. It was enormous, with heavy antique furniture, ornately framed portraits of military men on the walls, and thick velvet curtains, which were drawn across the windows. The gloom in here belied the glaring white sun outside. But I guess that was the point.

I heard doors open to my right, and General Pena appeared. He was in full dress but his sleepy eyes told me that I had awakened him from *his* siesta. He was a short, bald man, just past middle age, but he was powerfully built and his military carriage was impeccably straight.

I wanted General Pena to tell me the circumstances of General Rodriguez's disappearance, and I wanted to find out exactly what the contents were of the papers Rodriguez had been carrying. General Pena treated me with politeness, but unlike Lorca, he was excessively formal. As we talked it became clear that he felt the army and the army alone should be investigating Rodriguez's kidnapping, and that he resented Lorca's being put in charge of the investigation. That also meant that he resented me. I knew, however, that Pena must be under orders from the Minister of Defense, who had no doubt gotten his orders directly from the King. And the orders were to cooperate.

And cooperate he did, explaining to me in detail how Rodriguez's car had been stopped going between here and a military installation on the outskirts of town. Rodriguez's driver had been killed and the car itself was found riddled with machine gun fire. Neither the police or the army had found any clues near the car that might lead to the kidnappers, not even any fingerprints.

The papers that General Rodriguez had been carrying were ones that contained state secrets relating to the operation of Spain's military bases, and, more importantly, Spain's plan for the development of nuclear weaponry.

"So it would be possible for someone to construct a bomb from the papers Rodriguez was carrying?"

"Yes, provided they had the proper scientific expertise. Yes, I'm afraid so, Mr. Carter."

"Did anyone know that the General was carrying these plans?"

"No, not even the officers at the installation to whom he was taking them. It had all been arranged secretly, in consultation with the Minister of Defense. But not even the Minister knew exactly the day that they were to be delivered. He left them strictly in General Rodriguez's charge. I was the only person who knew General Rodriguez was carrying the plans that day, and he didn't even tell me until a few minutes before he left. It was a horrible coincidence that they picked *that* day to kidnap him."

It certainly was a horrible coincidence. Who knew what the terrorists would do with those plans? Our only hope was that El Grupo wouldn't know what they'd found, and that Rodriguez wouldn't break under torture and tell them. But even if Rodriguez didn't break, it seemed unlikely to me that it would take the group long to figure out what they'd come across. From what I could see El Grupo Febrero was a highly sophisticated, extraordinarily clever group of terrorists. If El Grupo could come up with the right equipment (perhaps from the Russians) it wouldn't take them too much time to put the nuclear plan they'd found into use.

I'd learned from General Pena what I wanted to learn, so I took my leave, and taxied back to the hotel. I hadn't rested since I left California, so I climbed into bed to sleep until my ten o'clock appointment. I hoped my dreams would be more pleasant than the waking nightmare surrounding me.

Calle de Arboles was a quiet residential street located on the outskirts of town. Its small stucco houses were lined up in an orderly fashion, and most had small yards in front. Lights shone from houses all along the street, and as I drove along in the Mercedes Lorca had given me to use, I occasionally heard the sounds of laughter and music coming from windows and open doorways. I cruised past two-thirty-five and saw a light coming from a front window. I turned the corner at the end of the block and parked the Mercedes on a side street, two blocks down from Arboles.

I headed back to Arboles on foot, but just as I was turning the corner onto the street I saw a large green van drive up and park directly across from two-thirty-five. I ducked behind a hedge at the end of the block and watched. After a few seconds a door of the van opened, and a light came on inside. What I saw in that van chilled me: there were four men and one of them was speaking into a walkie-talkie. This looked like a trap all right. One of the men threw a beer can onto the street, then closed the door again. I waited, but the men made no attempt to leave the van. Now I couldn't go in the front door of a house that was obviously being watched, and watched, I thought, for my arrival. But I sure as hell wanted to find out who was inside that house and what was going on there.

I looked around me, studying the layout of the neighborhood. Behind me, in the middle of the block was a narrow alley that had to lead past the back of two-thirty-five Arboles. I memorized the shape and color of the house, then, seeing that the men in the van still weren't ready to make a move, slid along the hedge until I came to the alley. The alley was very dark, and both sides of it were bordered by stucco walls taller than my head. I made my way to what had to be the right house. I checked back to see if anyone had followed me: the alley was deserted. I pulled Wilhelmina, my 9mm Luger, out of my breast pocket. I grabbed at the high stucco wall, gained a footing, and thrust myself to its top.

I found myself looking down into a small garden with a few orange trees, a bed of roses that looked like it needed tending, and a patio with two wrought-iron chairs. The back of the house was dark. I let myself down into the garden and moved around it, making sure that it was deserted. At the back door of the house, I could see into a small kitchen, very neat and orderly. The door from the kitchen into the rest of the house was closed. I tried the outside door. It was locked. The window into the kitchen was also locked, but its latch didn't look very sturdy. Holding the window's frame at the bottom, I pushed upward. Within seconds I could see that the latch was beginning to pull itself loose from the window, and I just hoped it wouldn't clatter to the floor or the table below the window when it came off. I gave a final heave, the latch broke, and the window opened with a whooshing sound. Unfortunately the latch fell onto the oil-cloth covered table with a thump. I hoped the noise hadn't been heard, but I didn't have any time to wait if it had. I climbed through the window, jumped across the table, and with Wilhelmina still in hand, went to the door leading into the rest of the house. I paused there. The only sound was the hum of the refrigerator. Who knew what or who was on the other side of the door? But I had to take that chance.

I turned the doorknob and opened the door a crack. Light from the next room flooded into the kitchen. Opening the door wider, I peered into a small living room, modestly and sparsely furnished. No one was in sight. Slowly I wedged through the door into the room.

"Drop it," a woman's voice on my right commanded.

I didn't drop it. I spun around and found myself

face to face with one of the most beautiful women I've ever seen. Her narrow, delicate face, her long black hair, and her large, soulful eyes made her look like a Madonna in a Spanish Renaissance painting. She held a small silver handgun, which was aimed right at my chest, as Wilhelmina was aimed at hers. We stood there several seconds, just staring each other down.

"Drop it," she finally said again.

"I could say the same. Are you the woman I talked to this afternoon?"

"I don't know what you mean."

"El Grupo Febrero?"

"I don't know what you're talking about," she said. But I recognized the soft, nervous voice. "Get out of here."

"You said this afternoon you had information."

"I don't know what you mean or want. Just please get out."

"Or you'll call your friends in from outside?"

Her face recoiled as I said this, as though she'd been slapped, and her arm with the gun jerked back. But the gun was still pointed at my chest.

"Your friends outside," I persisted, "in the green van."

She looked involuntarily toward the front windows, and I had my chance and moved rapidly. I knocked the gun out of her hand. As it clattered to the floor I reached out and grapped her with my left arm, pinioning her to my chest. She let out an involuntary cry, but she didn't struggle. She felt like a small, defenseless animal in my arms, and I don't like to hurt women, not unless I have to. But I knew those men were outside and I didn't have much time to make her talk.

"You called this afternoon," I said.

She didn't answer. I tightened my grip around her body.

"Yes, I called."

"So why lie about it?"

"Please," and she was crying softly by now. "Let me go. I'm afraid." I wanted to let her go, but I couldn't take any chances until I found out what she knew.

"Tell me about the men outside."

"I really don't know what you're talking about," she said through her tears. I released her, but kept her covered.

"I can't talk about El Grupo Febrero, please. I shouldn't have called. I really don't have any information." Her voice was pleading with me and it was filled with fear.

"Have you been threatened?"

She looked into my eyes for the first time. "Yes."

"If you talk?"

"Yes."

"How? Your life?"

"It's not just me, it's . . ." and her voice trailed away.

"Yes?"

But I didn't get a chance to wait for her answer, for just then I heard a door slam outside, and I could tell from the sound it was the van.

"Does the bedroom overlook the street?" I asked her.

"Yes, but . . ."

"Are the lights out in there, the shades drawn?"

"The lights are out, but . . ."

"Let's go." I took her arm.

"No, please, not in there," and she shied away from me. I knew what she was thinking.

"I'm not going to hurt you, but it looks like the men I mentioned are paying us a call."

She led the way down the hall to a small bedroom. We looked out through its darkened window. Four men had gotten out of the van and were crossing the street: an enormous man, almost seven feet tall and packed with muscles, seemed to be leading the way. Another of the men had a narrow scar across the length of his forehead as though someone had tried to scalp him and cut too low. All four were wearing blue jeans and work shirts.

"Oh, no," the woman whispered.

"Have you seen them before?"

"Only today. The man with the scar. I remember seeing him this afternoon."

"After you'd made the call to the police station."

She hesitated, thought for a moment. "Why, yes, it was near the phone booth that I saw him."

"Was he following you?"

"I don't know," she hesitated, looking out at the men again. "For the last few days I've felt as though I were being followed. I can't explain why, I didn't see anyone, but I just felt something." The men were now on the lawn.

"All right. Stay in this room. Don't come out under any circumstances." I handed back her gun, which I'd pocketed. "If anyone comes through that door shoot."

"I couldn't. I really didn't mean to shoot you.

It's not even loaded."

"Do you have any bullets?"

"In the bureau."

"All right. Get them. It's your life or theirs. Promise me you'll shoot at whoever comes through that door. And shoot to kill." She looked up at me, her eyes full of fear, but she nodded.

I rushed back into the living room, just as I heard the men's footsteps on the front porch. I moved to a position beside the front door, avoiding walking past the shaded windows. I didn't want them to see my silhouette.

The doorbell rang, a loud clattering sound. I held Wilhelmina and waited. The doorbell rang again, and this time whoever was ringing left his hand on, and the sound became an insistent, demanding shriek.

"She's got to be in there," I heard one of them say.

"Him, too?"

"I don't know. But she's there all right."

The leader, who must have been the tall man, told two of the men to go around and enter through the back way. Then suddenly there was a blast of gunfire that shook the door and sent the lock flying off its hinges.

The man with the scar entered first, his gun pointed out in front of him. I didn't let him get far. With my left hand I chopped down hard on his gun arm, sending the gun clattering across the tile floor, and with Wilhelmina I struck a clean blow against the side of his head, just below the ear. He crumpled to the floor immediately, out cold, as blood trickled from beneath his ear. I slammed the door against the big man coming in behind him, and took the few seconds this gave me to run toward the sofa on the opposite side of the room.

The big man was quick, though, and as I dashed a bullet whizzed past my head, missing by only a fraction of an inch. Another bullet whizzed by me, just as I ducked behind the sofa. Then I looked up to aim. He'd stationed himself beside a chair near the front window. As he looked up to see what his shots had done to me, I let loose with my first shot, but he ducked back down and the bullet hit the wall behind him. He sent another couple of shots toward me, and I could feel the chipped plaster behind me spinning off against the back of my head. I aimed again. One shot shattered the glass window just to the left of him, but the other grazed the side of his cheek. When he raised up to aim again, I went for his gun hand and landed on target, nicking the bone of his elbow. He howled with pain as his hand jerked back and involuntarily sent his gun crashing through the front window.

As I stood up to move toward him, I heard a noise to my left and turned just as one of the other men moved into the living room from the kitchen and sent a slug toward me. Only by throwing myself as quick as I could to my right did I miss that one. He raised his gun to aim again, which was his mistake, for without bothering to aim, I fired and hit him right between the eyes. As he fell, I fired at his friend coming from the kitchen, but he jerked back behind the door. It was then that I felt a bone-crunching blow on my right arm. Now it was Wilhelmina's turn to go crashing to the floor. As I whirled around I caught a severe blow on the right side of my neck and saw the big man standing before me, a poker iron in his hands. If I hadn't turned and glanced off the blow with my neck muscles, the back of my head would have been crushed to pulp. I staggered from the blow, but I managed to duck and miss as the poker came down again. I rammed my head as hard as I could into the big man's gut, and we both went crashing onto the hard floor. He still had the poker, though, and he brought it down on my back, temporarily knocking all of the air out of me. Then he was on top of me, with my throat pinioned beneath the poker.

"Get away from him, Carlos, so I can blast him," said his companion who had now come in from the kitchen. But Carlos wanted to finish me off himself and told his friend to find the woman. He pressed the grooved edges of the poker deeper into my throat, as I gasped for breath. And he leered to his companion, "Don't kill her off yet. She's real pretty and I know how to get information from the women." They both let out nasty laughs as Carlos' friend moved to the hall. My breath had now returned, and gathering up all my strength, I jabbed my knees up hard into Carlos's lower back, stunning him enough so that his grip loosened on the poker. This was the opening I needed to push the poker away from my neck. Carlos lost his balance as I pushed up, and we rolled across the floor, the poker now wedged between our chests. The poker's rough ridges were cutting into my flesh, as they were no doubt cutting into his also.

It was then that the woman screamed from the bedroom, and the scream was followed by a volley of shots. The woman's heartbreaking cry seemed to give me added strength, and I managed to slam my fist hard into Carlos's ribs. He reeled back and the poker slid out from between us. I darted to grab the poker just as I saw his hand pick up one of the guns that had fallen to the floor. "Don't move," he said and brought the gun to my face. "If you move, you're dead." And I would have been. I let the poker slip from my hand and quit struggling. He grabbed my right arm, the arm where I keep Hugo, my stilleto, and he brought the gun up to the left side of my face, only inches from my temple. He forced me onto my back and straddled me, his knees pressing into my ribs.

"Now, *amigo*," he whispered, "tell me what you want with the lovely lady here."

I had to stall. I had to try to keep alive and hope that he'd eventually loosen his grip on my right arm.

"She asked me to help her. She says she's being followed."

"You are from the police?"

"No, I'm a friend."

"You lie," he said, and his big ugly face creased itself into a savage frown. He brought the gun closer to my temple. I knew his finger was on the trigger, although he hadn't cocked it yet. I had to make a move before he cocked it or it was all over.

"And you are from El Grupo Febrero?" I asked him.

"El Grupo Febrero." He yelled it out and then broke into a maniacal laugh. "El Grupo Febrero, *sí*." Then his laugh stopped as abruptly as it had begun, and his face turned red with anger. "What do you know of El Grupo Febrero?" he shouted at me. I didn't answer. "Talk," he said, and pressed the gun with such force against my left temple that his whole body seemed to bear down on it. In bringing such force to the left side of my body, he slightly decreased the grip on my right arm and gave me the opening I needed. I jerked my wrist, Hugo slipped into my hand, and concentrating all of my strength in my right arm I broke his grip so quickly he didn't know what was happening. I went straight to Carlos's heart and plunged Hugo into its depths. His mouth opened in a silent scream and blood spurted from his chest into my face. I felt his body go rigid and knew that he was dead. If I hadn't paralyzed him on my first strike, my head would have been a mass of blood and bones scattered across the floor.

I threw Carlos's body off mine and ran to the hallway. The man lay there, blood coming from a wound in his forehead and from one of his eye-sockets. The eye was rolling down the side of his cheek. Blood on his shirt indicated he'd been wounded there too. I walked into the bedroom, not wanting to look at what he'd done to the woman. I flicked on the light and saw her sitting on the bed, tears rolling down her face. She was miraculously unharmed, although I could see a couple of bullet holes in the wall above the bed. Apparently, she'd hit him first, throwing his aim off balance. And then she'd kept firing. I took the small, silver gun from her hand and held her shaking body in my arms. I knew there was nothing I could say now. I cradled her head against my chest and stroked her long black hair, as she wept softly.

"Your name is?" she finally asked through her tears.

"Nick."

"I am Maria." And then she was silent again.

I looked out of the bedroom window and bolted from the bed. What I saw was the man with the scar climbing into the van. He'd obviously recovered from the blow I'd given him when he'd first entered the house, and while I was in here had decided to get away. I told Maria to stay here while I went after him and not to call the police unless I wasn't back in two hours. I didn't want the cops arriving before I'd had a chance to search the men myself. I hated to leave Maria alone here, but I had to go after scarface before he got word to his comrades about what had happened. I grabbed Wilhelmina as I ran through the living room. As I reached the yard I saw the van screeching down the street. I aimed for its tires, but just as I fired it turned the corner and my bullets went whizzing into thin air.

Neighbors had been attracted by all the gunfire, and I could see their heads peeping out of windows. Only a few, however, had ventured onto their lawns. A few doors down a teenage boy stood beside a motorcycle and looked in my direction. Every minute counted now, and I knew I could save a lot of time by taking the cycle instead of walking back to my car. I ran to the kid and told him to give me the keys to the cycle. He looked at the gun in my hand and the blood all over my clothes and face, and must have thought I'd shoot him too if he didn't. He handed me the keys without a word. I jumped on the bike, put the keys in the ignition, and started the motor.

"I'll return it," I called as I took off down the street. I turned the corner. Scarface must not have known yet that I was following him, because he was still in sight on the same road. The van was several hundred yards ahead of me, heading out of town.

By the time the van reached open country, on a winding narrow road, I had closed to a hundred yards of him, and was still gaining. Unfortunately, he must have noticed me following him then. He suddenly picked up speed, and I tried to keep up. As he increased speed, he began speeding crazily around every curve. My motorcycle was cornering fine, thank God for that, so as we went through a stretch of winding road, I kept gaining on him.

I had to follow him, and take him alive, I hoped. His three companions were now corpses. Maria and I had had to kill them, but it had been a bad break for us as well as for them. Because corpses don't talk, and what I needed on this case was someone who would talk, whether he had to be forced to or not didn't much matter. I very much wanted to take the man with the scar alive.

I saw now that the van had no license plates, so there wouldn't be anything to work on from that angle. If the man got away, I at least wanted to have some clue. I tried to pull up alongside him. In my pocket I had a tiny camera loaded with night film that would take a clear image of him if I could just get alongside him and aim it at his face. Unfortunately each time I approached his left he veered in that direction, forcing me back behind him again. He managed this on several curves until he met a slow-moving, mule-drawn wagon coming from the other direction.

He wheeled the van to the right. It skidded and came back to the left, catching the back of the wagon which was loaded with produce. The wagon tipped, then swayed back and tipped part of its contents into the road in front of me. I felt my wheels slide as I careened through a bunch of tomatoes, but I held on steadily and managed to get through the mess.

I was again right on top of the van. Again I tried to get alongside it, and again he veered to the left, heading me off. Then, with an enormous squealing of brakes and screeching of rubber, he braked as quickly as he could. His idea was that I'd run smack into the van and break every bone in my body. Thank God it took him longer to come to a complete stop than it did for me to react. In that fraction of a second I veered completely to the left and went off the road into a ditch. The bike went out from under me, and I landed in a field, several feet beyond the ditch. I felt a sharp pain all through my body, and lay, momentarily stunned, as I heard the van switch gears and pull off. I picked myself up, moving very gingerly. I ached, but I decided that at least there were no broken bones. I went to the ditch and dragged the cycle back to the road. Fortunately the earth had been good to it too. No major parts were broken, although the mirror was broken off and the windscreen was bent out of kilter. I cursed the distance between the van and me and hoped it wasn't completely out of sight. I jumped back on the cycle and took off.

Several minutes later I still hadn't picked up the

van. Then I heard an explosion from around a curve in front of me. The sky was illuminated in a flash, and I heard another explosion. Rounding the curve, I saw the van sitting on a train track. It had rounded the curve too quickly and run smack into a train, a train that must have been carrying gasoline. Another explosion sent billows of smoke and fire through the air. The fire rose high up into the sky. I could see the crumpled body of the van, now looking very black and very tiny against the huge orange flames.

"Corpse number four," I said to myself, and turned the motorcycle back toward town.

Chapter Three

By the time I got back, the neighborhood of Los Arboles had returned to normal. The neighbors who'd come out onto their lawns had gone back inside, and heads were no longer peering out of windows. The sounds of music and laughter wafted out of windows into the night air once again. I pulled up in the yard from which I'd taken the motorcycle. Hearing the sound of the bike's roaring engine, a head peeped out of a window. Then it quickly disappeared. I mounted the steps of the house and knocked. There was no answer. I guessed that the people who lived inside were still afraid of the madman with the gun. I knocked a second time, then a third, and finally the teenager from whom I'd taken the bike appeared at the window-pane in the door. But instead of opening the door, he moved his arms in an angry gesture, indicating that he wanted no further part of me. I could understand how he felt, but I held up my special Spanish Security badge and motioned him to come outside. I guess he recognized the badge or at least knew that it was something official, because he slowly opened the door and came out onto the porch. Other faces popped up in the doorway now and a woman, who must have been the kid's mother, shouted for him to get back inside, but he was already moving toward his bike.

I followed him and explained that I had been chasing criminals. This didn't seem to count much for him, though, as he surveyed the damage to his bike: the broken-off mirror, the bent windscreen, the scratched chrome and battered fenders. His face became a sullen mask of anger and disappointment. I pulled out enough money from my wallet to more than cover the costs of repairs. As I handed it to him, his face was suddenly wreathed in smiles. I returned his smile, remembering when I was a kid with a bike. As I walked down the block to two-thirty-five Arboles, the boy's shouts of thanks and good luck followed me.

At Maria's the front door was still open and I walked into the living room, noticing the two bloody bodies still on the floor. I called out for Maria.

"In here!" she called from the kitchen. I started toward the kitchen, then I stopped as I heard another voice from there, a low voice whose words I couldn't make out. I listened intently and made out still another voice: this one sounded like a woman's, but harsher, older than Maria's. What was going on? Had more members of El Grupo come? Were they holding Maria, even now, a gun pointed at her head? Was this another trap I was supposed to walk into?

I pulled Wilhelmina out of my pocket again, reloaded her as quietly as I could, and made my way slowly to the kitchen door. I stopped at the door and listened. Now there was silence.

"Maria?" I said.

"In here," she said again.

I cocked the gun, kicked the door open with my foot, and jumped into the room, covering myself.

Blood-curdling screams were let out by two women, one very old, one middle-aged, who were sitting with Maria at the kitchen table drinking coffee. I rapidly put down my gun, but not before the older had upset her coffee and nearly the entire table. I apologized, and Maria went to comfort the frightened old woman.

"It's all right," Maria said as she put her arm around the old woman's shoulder. "This is the man who helped me. He is from the police department." The old woman's fright turned into a shy smile of embarrassment, and the middle-aged woman let out a short, self-mocking laugh and nodded at me. Maria explained to me that the women were both neighbors who had come to stay with her while I was away, as the women vigorously nodded their heads.

"You've got to get out of here," I said to Maria. "When whoever sent those men discovers that they aren't returning—and they've probably already discovered it—more men are going to be coming here."

Both of the women said that Maria could stay with them. But I vetoed that. Maria needed to get out of the neighborhood for a while and go into hiding. Besides I still hadn't had a chance to question her. I told her I'd get her a room at my hotel. The two older women protested this suggestion ferociously, saying that it was highly improper for Maria to come to my hotel. They looked at me suspiciously: I'd become a villian once again. But Maria obviously understood the necessity of getting away.

"It's all right," she said to the women. There was a gleam of amusement in her eyes when she looked up at me and said, "I'll go."

She said good-bye to her friends and the women were crying as they left: they were obviously fond of her. When they were out the door I guided Maria past the bodies to her bedroom. She averted her eyes and I felt her tremble as she stepped over the man that she'd killed.

While Maria packed I phoned Lorca and explained the situation. He said he'd send a task force of special policemen to clean up the mess and watch the house. I agreed to meet him tomorrow morning, after I'd tried to get more information out of Maria.

In the living room I knelt beside the body of the big bruiser who'd come after me with the poker iron. His goon face, with the eyes still wide open in surprise, stared up at me emptily as I went through his pockets. I found nothing. Then I searched the man who'd fallen by the door, and again there was no wallet, no driver's license, not even a slip of paper that could give me some clue to his identity. If these were members of El Grupo, it was a smart organization all right, real professionals; they weren't taking any chances about leaving clues.

The man in the hall, the one Maria had plugged, also had nothing in his pants pockets. In his shirt pocket, however, I did find something: a match. But not an ordinary match. It was longer and thinner than a kitchen match, and except for the white head, it was a bright and shiny silver. I know about metals and by scraping the match's base and rubbing the extract between my fingers I confirmed my suspicions: it wasn't just a paint job on it's wooden base, but a coat of silver leaf. Curious.

"What do you have?" Maria asked as she appeared in the doorway, wearing a fresh black sheath dress and carrying a small suitcase.

"A match." I held it up. "Recognize it?"

"No," she said. "It looks very expensive. Like it came from a fancy restaurant or something."

"Yes, maybe it did. And maybe it will be a clue."

Then I heard police sirens in the distance, heading our way. I wanted to get Maria away before she had to answer the police's questions, so I took her suitcase and motioned her to follow me. I led her through the kitchen, out the garden, and into the dark alley behind the house.

"Thank you," she said, as we walked through the alley. She placed her hand gently on my arm.

"You're a brave girl," I said, and put my arm around her shoulder as we walked to my car, sheltering her from the now chilly mountainous air.

"Hungry?" I asked as we headed back toward the central section of Madrid.

Maria laughed for the first time that night and said, "Yes, I am. It's strange. After something like that happening the last thing in the world you'd think you'd want to do is eat. But yes. I'm starving."

I picked a fine old restaurant I knew off of the Puerta del Sol. As the maitre'd showed us to our table near a three-tiered fountain in the center of the room, heads turned: Maria was that stunning.

Not a man in the room could help looking up at her luxurious black hair, her pale ivory skin, her ripe and voluptuous body.

Over paella and wine I told Maria about my mission in Spain. After what had happened, I didn't see the point of keeping it a secret at this point. I did, however, skip over a lot of details, just giving her the broader outlines of the El Grupo Febrero affair (leaving out the part about the nuclear secrets) and my work with the Spanish Intelligence Force. I hoped that by letting her know as much as I felt I could, I would gain Maria's trust and that she in turn would feel she could trust me and tell me what *she* knew.

My openness and the wine did seem to relax her. I couldn't help noticing that as she became more at ease and more animated she became even more beautiful. As she told me about her life she at first avoided talking about the situation at hand, and I didn't want to push her into talking about it until the time seemed right. Maria told me that she had been working as a typist, but was studying to be a dress designer at night. She had grown up in a poor family and her father died when she was very young. Two years ago her mother had also died, and she and her older brother Pedro, who worked as a librarian, had moved into their present house. Maria's voice caught when she mentioned her brother and the animation briefly drained from her face. I suspected that here I might find a clue to her connection with El Grupo.

"Where was Pedro tonight?" I asked.

Her large black eyes filled with sorrow. "I don't know," she said, and then she immediately changed the subject. She began quizzing me about the fashion industry in the United States, and she outlined her own career plans. After she finished her studies at the Spanish Fashion Institute she wanted to begin designing clothes herself. At first she would sell these to the large Spanish department stores, then when she had saved enough money she would open a shop of her own. Eventually she hoped to branch out, and if she was lucky she would even be able to some day sell her clothes in America. Her face became even more animated as she told me about the hopes and dreams, and I realized that beneath her soft, classical beauty, Maria was a very modern and a very determined young woman. When she used the phrase "when all of this is over" in relation to her plans, I decided that now was the time to find out what was going on with her and El Grupo.

"And when did all your present trouble begin?" I asked.

She was silent. I was almost sorry I had asked the question, for it was sad to see the happiness drain from those dark eyes and to see her red lips tremble and form themselves into a pout. Her gaze turned inward, as though her mind were replaying what must be a nightmare experience.

Then she swallowed, as though downing her fear, and she said, "I guess it all began when my brother disappeared, over two months ago."

"How did he disappear?"

"That's just it. I don't know. One night, when I came back late from school, there was a note from him saying he would be away a few days. I was puzzled, but I didn't think too much about it.

Then, after a week, when he had still not returned, I began to worry."

"That would have been just before the first attack of El Grupo Febrero?"

"Yes," her eyes flashed, "but I'm sure my brother had nothing to do with that. I don't like the implication."

"So why did you call the police today? Isn't Pedro your connection with El Grupo?" I was hitting her hard, but I had to. She was silent for a long while. Finally she spoke again.

"Nick, let me explain to you about El Grupo Febrero. My brother *was* a member of El Grupo, many years ago. But it was not then what it is now."

"It was a secret organization, wasn't it?"

"Yes. My brother told me about El Grupo during the time he was going to their meetings. We were very close. You must remember that ten years ago another regime was in power. There were many injustices, which my brother was against, as am I. The power of the police and army was unchecked. There was no real democracy. People who did not believe what the government believed were imprisoned, some were even tortured. El Grupo was for a just and democratic society and for that reason opposed to that government. To have been anything but secret would have meant harrassment and imprisonment for its members. But at that time El Grupo Febrero was not a violent organization."

"Then it became one?"

"I do not know what happened. As I said, my brother often talked with me about the group's educational and social goals. Then the government to which the group was opposed fell. I assumed that the group disbanded when democracy came to Spain. There seemed no need for it after the present government came to power. I cannot remember my brother mentioning it again, except . . ." Her voice trailed off. After a brief silence she went on. "I have talked with my brother twice since he disappeared. About a week after he left I received a call. He seemed very frightened. He told me not to mention his disappearance to anyone. I asked him where he was. He said he could not tell me. He said he was being hunted."

"Hunted?"

"Those were his words. Then a week ago he called again. He asked me if I was being followed. I said no. Then, because of his previous connection to El Grupo Febrero and because I had read so much about them in the papers, I asked him if he was still connected with them. He hung up, without answering. Strangely, it was after this call that I began to feel that I was being watched. Maybe I just hadn't noticed it before. There was nothing definite, but I constantly felt people were watching me."

"Like at the telephone this afternoon."

"Yes."

"You don't know where your brother was when he made the second call?"

"I think, perhaps, Barcelona. When I picked up the phone an operator's voice began to say something like 'Bar', then immediately my brother's voice came on the line interrupting her. And we used to live in Barcelona. We moved here after my mother died two years ago, because Pedro got the job at the library in Madrid."

"So when Pedro was a member of El Grupo it was in Barcelona?" Maria nodded her head.

"Did you know any other members of El Grupo?"

"No, as I said, it was secret and I was very young at the time. I do not want my brother to get hurt, Nick. That is why I haven't called the police before. I was afraid the police would track down my brother, and that they would think him responsible for what has been going on, because he was once a member of the group. But I know Pedro. He could not be taking part in such horrible killings of innocent people."

I refrained from telling Maria that all kinds of people could become terrorists, even the most innocent seeming and even the most beloved brothers. I knew that Maria believed that Pedro wasn't taking part in the killings, and perhaps he wasn't, but there was clearly some connection between his disappearance and the emergence of El Grupo.

"I will do everything I can to keep your brother from being hurt, Maria, but only a bad purpose can be served by your hiding information from me. Innocent people are dying, the Spanish government is being destroyed."

"The only thing I remember about El Grupo," Maria said, "is one name. My brother often mentioned going to meetings at Dona Pretiosa's. I believe she had a shop or a bar or something in the Barrio Chino and that's where they held their meetings."

"That's all you know?"

"That's all I know."

This information excited me; it was the first concrete lead we had about someone who might be connected with the group. I told Maria that I would probably be heading for Barcelona to search for Dona Pretiosa and for her brother.

"Can I go with you?" Her eyes implored me. "If you do find my brother, I would like to be with you when you do—regardless of what he's done. And perhaps I can help prove his innocence."

Taking Maria with me didn't seem like a bad idea. She knew Barcelona better than I and might be able to help me find Dona Pretiosa. And—it was tough to think of it in these terms, but I'm in a tough business—if Pedro were a member of El Grupo and I had Maria with me as I looked for him, it was possible that he would come forward, if for no other reason than to get in touch with her. I told Maria I'd find out what headquarters thought of her plan, but that I would certainly like having her along—for a number of reasons.

"And I would like to be with you Nick—for a number of reasons." She smiled at me, and we looked deeply, longingly into one another's eyes.

I had already called the hotel from the restaurant to have them make up a room next to mine for Maria. I wanted to keep her as close as possible to me until I found out what Lorca would advise me to do with her. I unlocked her hotel door and set her suitcase inside, then let her pass into the room. Her pale face looked up at me and again our eyes met. I could feel the warmth of her body next to mine and smell her slightly musky perfume. I bent my head down toward hers, and her mouth opened for me. My tongue grazed her beautiful red lips, and then moved inside her mouth, exploring it. Her tongue met mine.

"You may come in," she said softly when we broke our embrace. I moved into the room, closed the door behind me, and took Maria in my arms. We kissed again, and I began exploring her firm, young body: the delicate arch of her back, her perfectly formed hips, her welcoming thighs. I unzipped her black sheath from the back and let my hands slide along the soft skin of her shoulders. Her dress fell to the floor, and she looked up at me with those huge, dark eyes, now gleaming with anticipation. I gazed, almost breathless, at her incredibly beautiful body, now naked except for a pair of black lace panties. Her long dark hair fell across breasts which were white as ivory and as inviting as any I'd ever seen. Her large rosy nipples strained out, already erect with excitement. I bent and took first one and then the other nipple into my mouth, kissing and licking them, and Maria let out a soft whimper like a little animal. I moved my hand to the jewel-like darkness beneath her belly and Maria moaned loudly. I lifted her to the bed and quickly undressed, then lay down beside her.

I moved my large body onto her small, delicate frame, and entered her with a slow, gliding movement. Slowly, slowly our rhythm built, until Maria grabbed frantically at my back and thrust her legs around my hips. We moved together creating a crescendo of passion. Then she let out one final, long groan of ecstasy.

We both lay breathing deeply for many minutes.

Then Maria gently stroked my forehead and said, "And to think that I was so afraid of you at first." She kissed my eyelids before snuggling into my arms, and we both drifted into a deep, satisfied sleep.

Lorca's pretty secretary was again bent over her fashion magazine when I arrived at Spanish Intelligence Headquarters the next morning.

"Good morning, Mr. Bryan," she said, smiling mockingly and, as she had yesterday, inflecting my cover name with a note of irony. She buzzed me through the steel doors, and Lorca rose from behind his enormous desk to greet me. He was cordial but unsmiling. He seemed worried.

"Before you give me your news of last night, Nick," he said, "let me give you mine. I hope yours is better—or, God help us, no worse, than mine." Lorca's whole face showed the strain of his job and of this whole bloody business. "Early this morning," he continued, "El Grupo Febrero sent out its latest communique. They left a tape—which is their usual method of relaying information, and, I might add, of taunting the police—outside a radio station near Seville. They must have left the tape there in the dead of night; no one saw it delivered. The station manager found it when he went to work this morning at six a.m."

"What do they say?"

"Listen for yourself. I have a recording of it here," and Lorca went behind his desk and pushed a button.

After a moment of static I heard the recorded voice of a fairly young man—probably somewhere between twenty-five and thirty years old—denounc-

ing the "imperialist, fascistic" government of
Spain. Then, in the name of El Grupo Febrero, he
claimed responsibility for the kidnapping of General Rodriguez, the "capitalist lackey" responsible
for many "crimes against the people of Spain."
Rodriguez would be tried for these crimes, the man
announced, at a special revolutionary tribunal,
which would commence tomorrow. Rodriguez's
crimes, as the voice on the tape outlined them, included causing unemployment, favoring the "dirty
rich," bilking the poor of their money to support
the army, withholding government secrets from the
citizens, "suppressing" civil revolution—that is,
keeping order and plotting with the United States
and other corrupt Western powers to keep the people of the world from having the revolutionary
governments they desired. The man explained, in a
cool reasonable voice which belied his wild accusations, that if found guilty of these crimes, General
Rodriguez would be sentenced to death and executed by El Grupo Febrero's "people's army."

"Not much doubt that he'll be found guilty, is
there?" Lorca remarked bitterly.

Then the man on the tape announced that he had
with him the man who was accused of these crimes,
and asked if the man had anything to say for himself. After a several second pause, an older man's
frightened voice spoke, saying over and over again
"No, no, I'm not guilty of what you accuse me of."
It was pathetic to listen to him forced to deny such
trash.

"That's definitely Rodriguez on the tape?" I
asked Lorca.

"Yes, I had my men at Army listen to it this

morning, it's him all right."

The "revolutionary's" voice finally interrupted Rodriguez's feeble protests. "The people, not you, lackey, will decide upon your guilt." Then there was another pause on the tape (apparently Rodriguez was being led away) before the spokesman of El Grupo began another harangue. The man promised that El Grupo Febrero would strike again by the end of the week. The band would not sleep until it had eliminated all of the enemies of the revolution. And this time they would strike "as high up as we can go."

"That's it," Lorca said, switching off the tape. "It seems El Grupo is getting more and more bloodthirsty. What does 'as high up as we can go' sound like to you, Nick?"

"They must mean the King."

"That's what I'm afraid of. I've already sent over an extra squad to the Palace, and I have extra guards assigned to the King at all times. I suggested that he cancel all his public appointments until this thing is cleared up. But he is a very courageous man. He wants to set an example to his people by carrying on as usual, and, of course, he's right to do so. It will show El Grupo Febrero that the government can't be bullied no matter how harsh the threats against it. Still, his safety worries me. We've *got* to get some lead on El Grupo soon."

"The tape itself offers no new clues," I asked.

"No, it's like all the rest of El Grupo's communiques. They're delivered in the middle of the night to some provincial radio or t.v. station or newspaper, when there's no one around who could see them. Each time it's a different place in a different part of the country—otherwise we could place guards. But we never know where they'll strike next. The tapes themselves, of course, never have any fingerprints, and they're on the kind of cheap cassettes you can buy in any record shop or drugstore in Spain."

"At least the tape didn't mention anything about the nuclear secrets. Maybe that's some comfort."

"Maybe, but then maybe not," Lorca said gloomily. "Perhaps they don't know yet what they have, perhaps they know and aren't mentioning it for reasons of their own. If they don't know yet, we'd better find Rodriguez before the trial and before they torture the information out of him." Then Lorca abruptly changed the subject, as though speaking of it was too painful. "So give me all the details of your adventure last night, Nick."

I described to him the events of the day before and I handed him the match I'd found on the dead man. Lorca said he'd immediately run a check on all the top restaurants and clubs of Madrid to see if he could trace the silver match.

"Try Barcelona too," I said. I told Lorca about Maria's conversations with her brother and about Pedro's disappearance. I handed Lorca the snapshot of Pedro that Maria had given me. It showed a pleasant-looking man in his late twenties who had Maria's pale skin and her large, dark eyes. Pedro was standing in a park, holding a balloon, hardly anyone's idea of a fearful terrorist.

"I'll have this blown up and sent across the country," Lorca said. "I'll put out an all-points alert for him. Even if he's not one of the terrorists, it sounds like he might be able to lead us to them."

Then I explained my plan to Lorca for having Maria accompany me to Barcelona to look for her brother and for Dona Pretiosa.

For the first time today a smile flickered across Lorca's face. "Your reputation with the ladies is legendary, but this is quick work indeed. In any case, it sound to me like a good idea for you to take Maria with you. I'll have my department check out the owners of all the coffee houses and bars in Barcelona and see if we can find one listed to Dona Pretiosa." Lorca paused and stared at me for a moment before going on. "By the way, Nick, I'd already made plans for you to go to Barcelona anyway."

My surprise must have been evident in my face, for Lorca laughed a short, bitter laugh. "Nozdrev," he said, "was spotted in Barcelona yesterday. I presume you recognize the name."

I recognized the name, all right. Mihail Nozdrev was my KGB counterpart. He was one of Russia's top agents, perhaps their best. For him to be in Barcelona forbode nothing but evil. It could well mean that the Russians already had a clue to what General Rodriguez was carrying on him. Already a deal might be brewing between the terrorists and the KGB. Even if the terrorists hadn't already contacted the KGB, it was more than an even bet that Nozdrev had arrived in Barcelona to convince them to play ball.

"You'll leave for Barcelona early tomorrow morning," Lorca continued. "I'm assigning a Spanish agent to assist you. You're to meet up tonight at a party given by Condesa Galdos. The agent will make contact." Lorca asked me now to

check with the photography unit and photo-
archives to see if they'd had any luck identifying
the men who'd attacked me last night.

"And good luck, Nick. Time is moving quicker
than we want. Stay in Barcelona as long as you
need to, but let me emphasize how grateful I'd be if
you can come up with something before this new
'trial' begins."

It was a tough order, but I'd do my best.

On the eighth floor I was greeted by Dr. Michez,
who showed me morgue photographs taken of the
men I'd killed last night. So far, he reported, the
photos didn't match up with any they kept in their
extensive archives—mainly photographs of con-
victed criminals and known menbers of subversive
organizations. He promised, however, to take the
men's photographs to the enormous archives of the
Army, where all of the men who had ever served in
the Spanish Army would have photographs and
other documents on file. Since most of the adult
men in Spain had, at one point or another, been in
the army, this looked like a promising avenue. The
only problem was the enormity of the archives. Dr.
Michez was taking along a bevy of researchers
with him, but it would still take a very long time to
comb through all of the back files. He promised to
work as rapidly as possible, including having a
team on twenty-four hours, and I thanked him.

I was discouraged though, that the researchers
hadn't already come up with something. In fact,
about the only good news so far today was that
Lorca had wholeheartedly agreed with me about
having Maria accompany me to Barcelona. On the
way back to the hotel I decided to stop and buy

Maria a present to celebrate our journey. I picked a deluxe French jewelry shop near our hotel. Inside I found just what I was looking for: a gold bracelet, simple yet elegant, that I knew would appeal to Maria's fastidious good taste. On the back of the bracelet I had them engrave:

"To Maria, thanks—for a number of things. N.C."

At the hotel desk I had a telegram from Hawk, which read,

Congratulations on latest contract. STOP.
Check out underground construction in Barcelona. STOP. Make sure to note height

which translated meant that Hawk had already found out about Maria from Lorca (for some reason he often referred to my women as "contracts"), that he wanted me to try my damndest to penetrate the secret (i.e., "underground") organization of El Grupo, and that he wanted to remind me that we were now playing for the highest stakes—possibly nuclear blackmail. Sometimes I felt that David Hawk knew more about my actions than I knew myself.

Upstairs I took Maria's bracelet out of its case. I wanted to surprise her by slipping it on her arm as I embraced her. I knocked. She didn't answer, which was strange, as I'd told her not to go out of the hotel under any circumstances. I knocked again. Still no answer. I turned the knob to her bedroom and the door opened. Then I felt as though a bomb had exploded in my brain, my heart, my groin. For Maria lay in bed, still naked from the night before. Blood seeped onto the white pillows, turning them pink, and formed a pool around the beautiful black hair. Maria's throat had been slit from ear to ear.

I looked down at the gold bracelet hanging limply in my hand.

Chapter Four

I quizzed the floor maid, the desk manager, the elevator operator, eventually the entire hotel staff that was on duty that morning. No one had seen anyone enter or leave Maria's room, and no one had noticed any suspicious-looking characters hanging around the hotel. Apparently El Grupo—if they were Maria's murderers—had changed their uniform for this assignment: anyone wearing jeans and a work shirt would have been noted immediately in the posh hotel where we were staying.

Assuming that El Grupo had murdered Maria, and I did assume this, I became less and less certain that her brother Pedro was taking part in their present bloody activities. There was no doubt that the present members of El Grupo were homicidal maniacs, but from what Maria had told me, and from what I learned about Pedro that day when I checked out his activities with some of his colleagues at the Madrid Library, Pedro just didn't seem to be the type.

Pedro had worked in the history division at the library. The head of this department, Dr. Diego Marquez, a scholarly-looking man in his late fif-

ties, told me that Pedro had always been reliable
and hardworking, an ideal employee. Pedro had
moved up rapidly in the library hierarchy since
coming there two years ago, and Dr. Marquez told
me that recently he had recommended that Pedro
be promoted to his assistant. Dr. Marquez had
been upset when Pedro hadn't shown up for work
two weeks ago, and had been even more upset
when he had called Maria and she had told him
that Pedro would be away from work for a few
days. But she couldn't offer any explanation. Several days later when he called Maria again, she had
said that Pedro was away and wouldn't be returning to work at all.

"I'm glad you're investigating this," Dr. Marquez told me. "You seem like a capable man to me.
I thought something was fishy, and I even thought
of calling the police. But I decided it was none of
my business, since Pedro's sister told me that he
was all right. I just hope we get Pedro back."

Pedro's immediate co-workers confirmed Dr.
Marquez's high opinion of him, and added the information that he was exceedingly kind and helpful
to people under him in his division. One young
man told about the time Pedro had stayed after
hours for a week, and until midnight on the last
day of the week, to help complete an indexing
project.

"Without Pedro's help," he said, "I wouldn't
have completed the indexing and would probably
have lost my job. Pedro is a real friend."

It turned out, however, that neither this young
man, nor Dr. Marquez, nor any of Pedro's co-
workers were his friends outside of the library. He

had never—despite his friendliness and generosity —confided in anyone at the library about his personal life. He had discussed his leaving with no one. And no one at the library was in a position to either confirm or deny any political activities Pedro might have been taking part in, or even to comment on his political beliefs: no one could ever remember his having discussed them.

To all appearances, Pedro was an ideal worker and citizen—except for a youthful, and perhaps understandable flirtation with radical politics. He was a loving brother and a highly-valued colleague. And yet it seemed obvious that he had some connection with a group of bloodthirsty madmen, intent upon the destruction of the Spanish government, and possibly capable of international nuclear blackmail. Could Pedro be one of those men in whom the seeds of destruction are sown early, seeds which grow—despite an apparently normal outward development—until they surface at last and are released in unexpected and bloody vengeance? Or was Pedro one of those revolutionaries —by no means rare—who cultivate the demeanor of good citizenship in order to better carry out their secret bloody plots? A classic wolf in lamb's clothing?

Or was it possible that Pedro, an ex-member of El Grupo, was trying to halt their present activities? If so, why hadn't he gone to the police with any information he had on El Grupo? Could there be two branches of El Grupo, both opposed to the state, but who were fighting one another for control of the organization? Would that explain Maria's untimely and unnecessary death?

When I returned to the hotel later that afternoon to change clothes for the evening, I immediately had the sensation on entering my room, that someone had been in there. Then I noticed a set of architectural drawings which I'd brought to Madrid as part of my cover. I'd left them lying on a desk across the room from the bed. The drawings were still there, but I could tell they'd been moved a fraction of an inch. Someone had been here. It wouldn't have been the maid, for she'd already come that morning to clean.

Whoever it was had been searching my room. That in itself didn't disturb me, for I had no secrets, nothing here to reveal my identity except as David Bryan, New York architect.

What did worry me was that my visitors were probably the same ones who'd visited Maria, who'd murdered her in the room next door. What did they have in mind for me? I began checking out the room. I went through all of the drawers. I looked under tables, under the bed, in the closet and in the shower in the bathroom. I sighted along the woodwork to see if there were any cracks or loose moldings. I found nothing unusual, and I'd almost given up the search when my eyes lighted on a small console table beside a lounge chair.

I knocked against the side of the table. It was not solid wood, but was hollow inside. I took a knife and traced its blade along the edges of the table's side panel. Then I put pressure on the panel and it unwedged easily, falling onto the floor. I shined a flashlight into the whole, and looked into the table's hollow base. I found what I was afraid I might: at the bottom of the table's hollow base sat a foot-long, rectangular package wrapped in brown paper.

I slowly lifted the package out of the table, being careful not to make any abrupt movements. I gingerly cut around the wrapping paper. My suspicions were confirmed. Inside was a black metal box. A faint ticking coming from the box was almost imperceptible to the ear. It was a bomb all right. I shuddered.

I would have liked to have called Lorca and had him send over a squad of detonation experts, but I knew there probably wasn't time for that. The bomb had the kind of sophisticated triggering system in which you couldn't tell from the outside what time the explosion was set to go off. By the time Lorca got the experts here, I, and the people in the hotel rooms above and below and to the side of me, might already be blown to smithereens.

I went to the windows and looked out, hoping I could toss the bomb out that way. My room overlooked a shaded courtyard and fountain at the back of the hotel. Normally the courtyard was deserted, but today a group of people, who looked like English tourists, had decided to have cocktails out there by the fountain. Why had they picked this particular day to enjoy the courtyard's shaded recesses?

I now had two choices. I could make a run for it and maybe save my own skin. But that wasn't going to save the people in the hotel rooms around me. My second choice was to try to detonate the bomb myself, even though I knew it could blow up in my face at any second.

I made my choice. I got the appropriate tools

from my bag and steeled myself. I'm not a detonation expert, but I have some training, and this was my only hope of preventing another large-scale massacre by El Grupo. First I unscrewed the black metal base and removed it. Inside, next to the innards of the bomb, was the timer itself. My heart leaped against my chest: the timer was set to go off in less than one minute.

I studied the bomb itself. At first it looked completely unfamiliar, but then gradually, working back in my memory, I was able to find the various parts that corresponded to the parts of the bombs I'd already worked on. The structure of the bomb became comprehensible, and I decided the triggering device must be the tiny steel lever sticking out toward the timer.

Only a few seconds were left. If I pressed the lever in the wrong direction, everything would be all over. If I waited any longer, though, everything would be all over anyway. It was a question of do or die. I moved a pair of metal clippers to the lever and gritted my teeth. One quick motion jammed the lever to the left.

The ticking stopped. I smiled down at the clippers in my hand. I'd foiled their plot to have me follow Maria to the grave.

Spain has over 1,500 castles, and the Castle Galdos had to be one of the most spectacular. Sitting in park-like grounds along the Manzanares River, it was an enormous Romanesque structure of beige marble and red tiles. Lights glittered from four stories of windows as I pulled the Mercedes into the circular driveway and stopped the car beside a large, round fountain in front of the main entrance.

A man in black and gold livery helped me from my car, and inside the house a butler checked my name against a large guest list. I'd been invited here ostensibly because of my interest in Spanish architecture, and because Castle Galdos was one of the outstanding structures in Spain of its particular period. In fact, Lorca had told me that a number of high government officials would be attending the party here, given by La Condesa Galdos, the widow of a government minister. He wanted me here in case any trouble developed and because it was a convenient place for me to meet up with my Spanish contact. Lorca had told me he was taking extra security precautions because of the distinguished guest list, and I noted four Spanish officers in full dress flanking the castle's ballroom entrance.

"Mr. David Bryan of New York City," another liveried attendant announced as I descended the steps into the enormous gold and white ballroom.

Heads turned briefly to look as I moved down the marble stairs, then turned back to their companions to chatter. A few people, mainly women, followed my entire descent. I smiled at a shapely redhead who was staring at me from across the room, and caught the eye of a statuesque brunette.

Reaching the bottom of the stairs, I surveyed the crowd. They were a glittering lot, all right, a combination of la crème de la crème of Madrid society and the highest officers of the Spanish government. The men were, for the most part, a distinguished-looking lot and carried themselves with that air of authority and complacency of the very powerful. All of the women were beautifully dressed, and many of them were, simply, beautiful, exquisite in that way that only wealthy women with the means and the leisure to pamper themselves endlessly are. It was difficult to believe, as I watched these people dancing and chattering gaily, that they were a group under siege, that the lives of who knew whom among them were in danger. And who in the crowd, I wondered, was the Spanish agent I was to contact?

I felt a hand on my right elbow.

"Mr. Bryan, I presume?" said a tantalizingly feminine voice.

I turned to my right.

There's a myth that all Spanish women—and particularly the most beautiful ones—are dark and diminutive, with brown eyes and black hair. The woman before me proved that the myth was totally wrong. Her hair, drawn back sleekly from her face, was ash-blond, and her complexion was tawny, roses and beiges mixed together in a delicious blend. Her eyes were of a cool but intense green. And she wasn't small. She was cast in the heroic mold, only four or five inches shorter than me. Her statuesque curves were accentuated by the tight-fitting, low-bodiced evening gown she was wearing. Could *she* be my Spanish contact? I smiled at her, delighted at the prospect.

"I am your hostess," the woman said. "La Condesa Galdos."

I was dismayed that I wouldn't be working with this beauty, and I was surprised that this was "the widow of an ex-government official" Lorca had described to me. I'd expected someone at least fifty, with a heaving bosom, and weighted down with jewels.

These two reactions must have both played momentarily on my face, for La Condesa smiled mischievously and asked, "Is anything wrong, Mr. Bryan?" Her voice was low, throaty, and incredibly sexy. "Perhaps," she continued before I had a chance to answer her, "you were expecting some other type of person. People often do. My late husband was twenty-five years older than I. People sometimes expect me to be of his generation." La Condesa had read my thoughts all right.

"Perhaps," I said.

"Well, no cause for dismay, I hope?" Again she smiled at me mischievously.

"No cause whatever." I smiled, looking at the large emerald necklace, hanging against the soft, tawny skin of her voluptuous breasts.

At this point La Condesa and I were interrupted by some of her other guests, an older, very thin, gray-haired woman, the Princess of Sedula, and a small, fiercely elegant, extremely handsome man of middle-age, El Conde Ruiz. La Condesa responded charmingly to the Princess's effusive greetings, and smiled—cordially, but also with a hint of irony—at El Conde Ruiz. The social chatter between El Conde—who explained to me that he was a former government official and ex-officer of the army—and La Condesa was pleasant and affectionate, but I sensed a tension beneath the surface pleasantries, as though they were really speaking to one another about something completely different from their ostensible subjects. As they chatted with the Princess about the latest art shows and parties of Europe, I excused myself. Their blood was too blue

for me. Besides, I needed to be alone if my Spanish
agent was to approach me with any kind of discre-
tion.

"Perhaps you would care to stay later," La Condesa whispered to me, "so that I can show you the
various other parts of the castle. The Minister of
Culture tells me you're here surveying Spanish
architecture." Did I detect a scowl, quickly covered
by a smile, pass across Ruiz's face as she said this?
I told La Condesa that I'd like very much indeed
for her to "show me the castle," and went off to
look for my Spanish agent.

I was heading toward the bar on the other side of
the room, when a great murmuring went up among
the people surrounding me. They were all turning
toward the ballroom's entrance. As I turned to see
what was happening, I heard the blast of a
trumpet. At the top of the staircase I saw what everyone was excited about. There stood an attractive young couple. As the liveried servant announced, "The King and Queen," the couple
began descending the staircase. Suddenly everyone
was silent, and I noticed La Condesa move to the
bottom of the stairs to greet her new guests. She
embraced the King and Queen as though they were
old and close friends, and then the three of them
and half a dozen others in the royal party moved to
the side of the ballroom and formed a reception
line. Guests began filing past them. I figured this
was one ceremony I could skip. I was more interested in saving the King's government than in
making small talk with him.

During the next hour a number of people approached me, mostly women, and I talked

amicably with them about my architectural research in Spain and satisfied their curiosity about
current happenings in New York and Washington.
Nearly everyone I spoke with mentioned her anxiety about El Grupo; contrary to appearances, the
subject was on everyone's mind. But no one identified himself or herself as my co-worker.

I was talking with Manuel Ricardo, the current
Minister of the Treasury of the Spanish Government, about a mutual interest, Moorish architecture, when I happened to glance toward the windows near us, which faced onto a terrace overlook-
ing the Manzanares River. What I saw shocked the
hell out of me. Standing behind a French window
was a figure I couldn't make out. But what I could
make out was the XM pistol the figure was holding. The metal of the gun reflected the light of a
candelabra. Whoever was holding the pistol out
there in the dark must have seen me looking, for a
slight jerk of the pointed barrel indicated that the
pistol was being cocked. Without thinking, with
only a visceral reaction, I threw myself toward
Manuel Ricardo, plunging my head into his stomach, attempting to throw both of us to the floor.
But it was too late, the bullet came whizzing toward us, missing my head by a fraction of an inch,
but plunging straight into Ricardo's heart. A tiny
jet of blood spurted onto my forehead, and a small,
gurgling sound came from the Minister of the
Treasury's throat. By the time we hit the floor I
knew that he was dead.

Whoever fired the gun had used a silencer, so at
first the other guests didn't know what had happened. When, however, I rose, and people near us

saw the blood on my head and then the red seeping through Ricardo's white shirt, pandemonium broke out. At first a few, then many women's shrieks burst out across the room as the news spread, and men and women were both scurrying across the room like rats trapped in a lethal cage, unsure of which direction to turn in. It was rough going shouldering my way past the pushing and shoving crowd to reach the terrace from which the shot had come. It was a waste of all too precious seconds.

I unpocketed Wilhelmina as I opened the French doors and stepped into the cool of the night. As I'd expected, the tile terrace was deserted. I looked over the marble balustrades—below was a straight drop of about a hundred feet to the Manzanares River. The terrace was closed to the left by a wing of the castle. To the right, marble steps led to a side garden. I went down these into the dark.

"Stop," a voice cried out, and I froze. "The police," the voice said a minute later. "Drop your gun and put your hands above your head." I did as I was told, and through the darkness three uniformed men came running toward me.

"I'm from the Special Security Force," I said and reached toward my pocket for my identification.

"Keep your hands above your head," said the man who was apparently the leader, as he fired a warning shot in the air. I put my hands back above my head. It's dangerous to mess around with cops who don't know what they're doing and have a gun pointed at you. The leader motioned one of the other men to search me. The man did so, murmuring "assassin" under his breath. I heard his intake of breath, however, when he found my identification. He immediately scurried to his superior, who, after glancing at the identity card, broke into loquacious apologies.

These were beside the point. It was now too late to look for anyone in the garden. If the assassin had come through the garden, he would have long since escaped under cover of my "capture."

"Wasn't anyone guarding this terrace?" I asked. "Weren't all entrances and exits supposed to be covered?" I heard the cold fury in my voice.

One of the guards looked down at his shoes and finally admitted sheepishly that he'd been stationed on the terrace steps, but had gone around the house—briefly, he assured us—to get a cigarette. When he heard the confusion inside, he'd been on the other side of the building. When he'd returned to this side of the building—with his buddies in tow —they'd found me coming down the steps. The man's superior now let loose with a torrent of abuse and obscenities, and I turned to go back into the castle. Heads would certainly be rolling at police headquarters tonight.

In the ballroom, the pandemonium had quieted down. La Condesa was moving among the guests, calmly reassuring them, apparently in complete charge of the situation. Now everyone was as silent as though they were at a funeral, which I suppose they were, in a way. A police officer informed me that the King and Queen had been surrounded by their private security force when the panic broke out, and had been whisked out of the castle immediately. Police photographers were now clicking away at the body of Ricardo on the floor, as the guests filed rapidly but quietly toward the entrance to leave.

I answered a few of the police's questions about what I'd seen, and then I moved to the entrance hall to watch the guests file out. Perhaps my Spanish contact would greet me as he or she left.

No such luck. At the end of another half an hour, all the guests had filed past La Condesa, an ambulance crew had arrived and removed Ricardo's body, and even the investigating officers had departed. But my agent hadn't made contact.

La Condesa Galdos, still calm as could be, approached me.

"So you are staying for your tour, after all," she said. "I'm afraid I must apologize. Usually my guests are not treated so badly. At least when they first visit."

"You were a pillar of strength," I said to her admiringly. Her sober countenance broke into a grin, and she laughed a deep, throaty laugh. I guess I looked puzzled again for she explained, "You have made, without knowing it, Mr. Bryan, a pun. A bilingual pun. My Christian name is Pilar, please call me that. Now come, your tour."

"Perhaps another time would be more convenient for you," I said. There was no reason for me to stay here now. I needed to get back to Lorca and find out what had happened to the Spanish agent. Much as I would have liked to spend more time with La Condesa.

"I think you had better let me give you the tour," she said. She took my hand. "Come along, Mr. Bryan, the dimensions of the castle are shrinking." That was it, "the dimensions of the castle are shrinking," the code phrase Lorca had given me. So I had been right after all. I looked at her, shaking my head in joy and disbelief: La Condesa, Secret Agent.

Over coffee in the Castle Galdos's library, I confided to Pilar that I was fairly certain the shot in her ballroom had been aimed at me, and not at Minister Ricardo. Although the guests, of course, and even the police had taken this as another of El Grupo's assassinations, it didn't look like El Grupo's style to me: no dramatics, no torture, so far no threats.

What neither Pilar nor I could figure out was how anyone could have got past the tight security force Lorca and the police had set up. The party hadn't been catered, but served by Pilar's own staff, which, she assured me, consisted, for the most part, of old family retainers, all of whom were infinitely trustworthy.

It was possible, of course, that the assassin had gotten wind of the party and entered the grounds of the estate by boating down the river and climbing up the steep bank and over the walls. The police had already put out a checkpoint for the boats along the river. But that approach would have taken a lot of planning, and if the assassin were after me, he couldn't possibly have had time to hire a boat and get there that quickly.

The other possibility was that the killing had been an inside job, either by one of the guests or by one of the security men. The latter possibility seemed extremely unlikely. So Pilar produced her guest list and we went over it, hoping that we could find some clue there. All of the people on the guest list, though, were eminent, most of the men high government officials, the women their wives, daughters, or themselves in positions of government trust and responsibility. Of course, there were, as Pilar pointed out, a number of people who could have been political enemies of Minister Ricardo. That is, people who opposed his policies. But hardly, one would think, opposed them enough to assassinate the man. The police had a guest list in their possession and would be investigating all this, but it seemed unlikely to me that the gunman really had been aiming at Ricardo and not me. And yet, supposedly, no one at the party had known who I really was except Pilar. It was a puzzle.

"And how did you get into this line of work," I asked Pilar.

She hesitated.

"Complicated explanation?" I asked her.

"No, not so complicated," she replied. She explained that she had been married—ten years ago, while still a student—to El Conde Galdos. El Conde came from one of the oldest and richest of Spanish noble families, but when Pilar met him he had been a professor of social sciences at the University of Madrid. She had been his student. Despite the difference in their ages, Pilar and El Conde had fallen deeply in love. Pilar came from a long line of anti-fascists. Two of her uncles had died fighting on the loyalist side in the civil war. And the Galdos family also, despite their wealth and aristocracy, had been anti-fascists. This had been one of the bonds between Pilar and the man who became her husband. Together the two of them had fought, as discreetly as possible to bring democracy to Spain. Shortly after the King came to power, he had asked El Conde Galdos, an old friend, to join his government, and El Conde had given up his professorship to become the Minister of Social Services.

"My husband was an idealist," Pilar said proudly, "and he was on fire with the idea of using his position to help the people—the poor, the peasants, the political outcasts like ourselves—who had suffered so long."

Galdos had died of cancer only a few months after taking office. At first Pilar had been almost inconsolable with grief, but soon she pulled herself together and realized that the best way to serve her husband's memory was by helping the regime they both had so many hopes for. But what could she do?

The idea of being an agent had occurred to her one day when Pilar was lunching with my boss, Lorca, who was an old school friend of hers. When she first proposed it, Lorca had scoffed.

"But I am persistent," Pilar said smiling, "Finally, I won him over. After all," she laughed, "who could have a more perfect cover? Who would suspect a rich, frivolous society lady of being a government agent?"

Pilar was mocking herself, but I knew she had to be damn good. She'd only been with the agency for two years. Yet for Lorca to assign her to an important case like this meant that she was already one of his top agents.

The phone rang in the room next to the library, and Pilar excused herself to answer it. When she returned to the library, her face was grim.

"That was Lorca," she said, "we are to proceed to Barcelona tomorrow as planned. Half an hour ago, a radio station in Catalonia received a new communique from El Grupo Febrero. They claim responsibility for the political assassination of Minister Manuel Ricardo."

Chapter Five

Naturally, all the newspapers the next morning played up the assassination of Minister Ricardo. They dwelt at length on the fact that the King and Queen had been in attendance at the party where he had been killed, some even going so far as to speculate that the bullet had been aimed at the King (despite the fact that the King and Queen had been completely across the room from Ricardo when the shot was fired). Ricardo's death was a gigantic propaganda coup for El Grupo, and a major embarrassment to the police and government. You could sense an electric wave of shock and panic sweeping through the Spanish populace.

Pilar and I set off for Barcelona that morning in the Mercedes and arrived in the city in mid-afternoon. After checking into a hotel off the Ramblas, we immediately set off for the Barrio Chino to search for Dona Pretiosa.

The Barrio Chino is an ugly, decadent part of Barcelona, not the kind of neighborhood where you'd be likely to stroll at night. Even during the day the place is dark because of the shadows the crowded buildings cast on the narrow, angular streets. Pickpockets and thieves lurk here, under cover of darkness, and even in mid-afternoon whores stand on doorsteps and lean out of windows, calling out raucous propositions. Drug dealers and peddlers of blackmarket goods hawk their wares on corners and stoops. From the open doors of bars and brothels, the sounds of cheap music and tired, argumentative voices waft onto the streets.

Lorca's agents had located one Don Santillana for us. Santillana ran a saloon called *La Cuchuracha*, one of the Barrio Chino's lowest dives, sort of a center for neighborhood crime. Santillana would know most of what was going down in the Barrio's streets and backrooms, and with luck he'd also know where we could find Dona Pretiosa.

La Cuchuracha was located in a large, dark basement room that we entered through a narrow alley. Already, although it was not yet nightfall, the room was filled with rough-looking types, and the air was heavy with the smells of alcohol, tobacco, marijuana, and opium. Tough and jaded-looking faces turned toward Pilar and me as we entered. Men's eyes drank in Pilar's beauty greedily, eyes that were used, I knew, to seeing only the most battered and hardened kinds of women. I couldn't help noticing that the only other woman in the bar was a slatternly barmaid, heavily made-up, and vulgarly dressed, who was serving drinks to a group of men at a table across the room. One of the men at the table whispered something in the barmaid's ear, and with a large lascivious grin on her face the woman made her way across the crowded room toward Pilar and me.

"I am Rosa," the woman said. She grinned, showing badly cared for teeth. "One of my friends wishes to buy you a drink," she said to Pilar. "And he asked me to ask your price." There was contempt in her voice, mockery in her flashing eyes.

"Tell your friend," Pilar said, not batting an eye, "that my price is much too high for him and that I do not drink with swine." Then Pilar fixed Rosa with such a cold, withering glance that the mockery drained from the woman's face and she immediately scurried back across the room, like a badly frightened hen. I had to hand it to Pilar. She might have been high born, but she certainly knew how to handle herself in places like this.

Pilar smiled at the man across the room, as the barmaid bent to tell him what Pilar had said. Then the big bruiser, who looked to be in his mid-twenties and already a seasoned criminal, rose and lurched toward us. I tensed as he made his way across the room, and took Pilar's hand in my own as he approached. The man swayed above us, obviously stoned on drugs or booze, and, ignoring me, went to Pilar and put his hand on her bare shoulder (she was wearing a tank top). I started toward him, but Pilar's reaction was even swifter. As cool and efficient as a machine, she removed the man's hand from her shoulder, then dealt him a blow on the chin with the back of her hand that sent him reeling toward the bar. The other people in the bar, who had been watching all this avidly, gasped at her effrontery and her strength.

I knew that a fight was on, for the man's four buddies had already risen from their table and were running toward us. For a moment I thought the whole *La Cuchuracha* crowd might join in the fray; they collectively shifted in their chairs as though getting ready to leap up. But they must have decided, at least until they knew what direction the fight would take, to sit back and see what would happen. They must have figured the five men would pretty quickly beat me to a bloody pulp, then have their way with Pilar.

"Pimp," yelled the first of the quintet as he came lunging toward me. I caught the weight of his body as he barrelled into me and with one motion threw him over my head. He flew through the air briefly then landed with a thunderous whack as he hit the ground; he was out. A second man rammed his fist into my stomach as the first went over, but my stomach is in pretty good condition, like steel, and I knocked this one out cold with a single punch against his jaw. Meanwhile Pilar had already jumped up as the original tough approached her again, and with a quick karate kick sent him whirling once again toward the bar. This time Pilar used such force that the man hit the steel covered bar with a bang and crumpled to the floor.

Already another man had grabbed Pilar's long blonde hair and was violently pulling on it, as though trying to wrench it from her scalp. He reached toward her breasts with his other hand, leering and growling "prostitute" as he did so. But before the hand could caress her breast Pilar kneed the man in the groin hard, and he involuntarily let go of her and howled with pain. While he was still stunned from this blow, Pilar picked up a chair and brought it down hard across the man's shoulders

and neck. The chair splintered as it struck, and the
lecher collapsed beneath its impact.

While this was going on, the last man had come
up on me from behind, pinioning my arms to my
side and clinging to my back like a monkey. Then
he moved one of his hands from my arms to my
throat and began squeezing hard. That was his mistake. I swiveled to my right, and with my now free
elbow I jabbed him just below his ribs. I heard the
whoosh of air as I knocked the breath out of him
and felt his grip on my throat loosen. With him still
clinging, now precariously, to my back, I propelled
us both backward with all my force. I heard the
crack of bone against wood as his head hit the wall
behind us, then he went completely limp and
slipped down my back like water.

The other customers in *La Cucharacha,* who had
been following this melee in attentive silence, now
unexpectedly let out a chorus of loud whoops and
whistles for Pilar and me. I guess they'd enjoyed
the fight and decided not to take us on themselves.
This ovation was still going on when I heard the
sound of shattering glass. Turning around, I saw
the barmaid Rosa weaving toward Pilar. The
jagged edge of the broken whiskey bottle in Rosa'a
hand was aimed right at the back of La Condesa's
neck. I yelled and Pilar turned just in time to avoid
the bottle coming toward her. Suddenly the crowd
was silent again.

I decided not to interfere. Rosa, unlike her
drunken cohorts, had a weapon that was, or could
be, lethal. She was armed and Pilar wasn't. But I
could see by now that Pilar could more than take
care of herself. The two women stood facing one

another. Then Rosa swung with her bottle again,
this time aiming at Pilar's throat. Pilar sidestepped
the blow, and as Rosa's arm came down, Pilar
grabbed it at the wrist. Pilar's grip must have been
strong, because the woman whimpered and let go
of the bottle, which crashed to the floor. With her
free hand, the barmaid grabbed at Pilar's waist,
knocking them both off balance. They fell to the
floor in a heap, and then they struggled with one
another as they rolled around on the floor, now
Rosa, now Pilar on top. Pilar soon, however, had
the frowsy barmaid beneath her.

"Not a very nice thing to do," Pilar said coldly,
looking down into the woman's furious face.

"Dirty whore," Rosa said as she went for Pilar's
eyes with her long red fingernails. But Pilar
checked the barmaid, dealing a swift, clean blow to
the side of Rosa's neck that put the barmaid out of
commission, at least temporarily.

Pilar rose, as cool as could be, smoothed her
clothes, and reached toward her purse. From this
she took a comb and straightened out her long
blonde hair. This gesture sent *La Cucharacha's* pa-
trons into an ovation that topped the first one. Apparently the men enjoyed a cat fight even more
than a fist-swinging free-for-all. A faint, ironical
smile played on Pilar's beautiful face.

"Drinks for all!" I turned to see that the booming voice came from an enormously fat, completely
bald man who stood beside the bar. The man
nodded at a couple of attendants who quickly
moved toward two of the recumbent figures on the
floor. As they hoisted the limp bodies over their
shoulders, then threw them into the alley outside

the bar, the fat man moved toward Pilar and me, beaming. This had to be Don Santillana, and I was glad *La Cucharacha's* manager had apparently enjoyed the fight as much as his customers.

"You begin fights in my bar?" Don Santillana said with mock severity. Then his face broke into a broad grin, and his huge belly shook as he laughed. With a wave of his hand, Santillana shooed away the group at the nearest table and invited Pilar and me to sit down with him. A bartender appeared immediately with drinks for all of us, and Pilar and I introduced ourselves, using false names. We told Santillana that we hoped he could help us locate Dona Pretiosa. The smile faded from Santillana's face and was replaced by the shrewd, calculating frown of a businessman. He said he didn't know a Dona Pretiosa in the neighborhood, but he might be able to have his men inquire about her whereabouts. Of course there would be a small fee. I pulled out my wallet and handed Santillana the Spanish equivalent of two hundred dollars.

"I will have my men begin making inquiries." Then he beckoned one of his lackeys toward the table. "Locating her will probably cost, however, more than this," he said, pocketing the two hundred dollars.

I motioned away Santillana's lackey as he came up to our table. I had a feeling Santillana already knew where we could find Dona Pretiosa. I didn't mind giving him and his men more money, but we didn't have time to play these elaborate games with him.

"Cut the crap," I said, and I explained that we had been sent here by the Barcelona Commissioner

of Police, and that we were working with the police
on the El Grupo murders.

I don't think Santillana was much impressed by
my bringing up the Police Commissioner, but he
was plenty impressed when I mentioned El Grupo.

"El Grupo," he said angrily and spat on the
floor. "They're a vicious group of hoodlums."
Which was pretty ironical coming from one of the
bosses of the Barrio's underground. "They disrupt
order," he went on. "They disrupt the Spanish way
of life. They make trouble for my business. The police enter the barrio, frightening my men, but we
have no connection with these scum. I am a businessman. I want to keep order. I want to see these
thugs destroyed." To emphasize his last point Santillana brought his fist violently down against the
table.

"Why didn't you tell me you two look for this
group. I cooperate with the police on this matter.
For this there is no charge. I pay *you* to find them."
Santillana pulled the two hundred I'd given him
out of his pocket and handed it back to me. He also
tried to get me to take an additional two hundred,
which I waved away. He raged for a few minutes
longer about El Grupo, then he gave us the information we'd come for.

Dona Pretiosa had run a small coffee house in
the Barrio for years. She had never had any connection with the organized criminal life of the Barrio, or "our business" as Santillana called it. Dona
Pretiosa was quiet, never caused anyone any trouble, and Santillana and his gang had left her and
her coffeehouse alone.

"A mistake, I now see," he said, shaking his

head. "I should have suspected something was up, all those dirty students and puny young men always in and out of her coffeehouse. They're not real men. I should have known they were filthy anarchists. We've been harboring them in our midst. We'll demolish the place," he said angrily.

Pilar and I had to persuade Santillana that it was extremely unlikely that Dona Pretiosa's coffeehouse was the headquarters of El Grupo, and that we merely wanted to question her because we thought she might offer us a few clues to the case. We explained that Dona Pretiosa herself was probably not involved. I didn't know whether this was true or not, but I certainly didn't want Don Santillana and crew barging in on her, and finally he agreed to leave Dona Pretiosa to us. He wrote down the address of her coffeehouse, and Pilar and I rose to leave.

"Destroy them, destroy them," he shouted as we left *La Cucaracha*.

Dona Pretiosa's small, candlelit coffeehouse was almost deserted. At the front of the cafe, a young girl with long dark hair was playing a guitar and singing a Spanish folk song. A couple sat at a table near her, sipping coffee, smoking cigarettes, and listening. Pilar and I were the only other customers. We sat down at a small, wooden table, several feet from the singer and were approached by a large, dark woman of middle years. We ordered *cafe cortado*, and the woman asked us if we were tourists. Pilar said that we were from Madrid.

When the woman returned with our *cafe cortado* I asked her if she was Dona Pretiosa.

"Yes." She smiled. Her eyes were warm and friendly. "Have friends in Madrid sent you to look me up?" she asked. Her voice was solicitous, that of a gracious hostess.

"We are friends of Maria Salas," I said, carefully watching Dona Pretiosa's face in the candlelight to see what effect the name had on her. Her smile did not fade, but her eyes seemed to cloud over with anxiety.

"I'm afraid I don't recognize the name," she said.

"She is the sister of Pedro Salas," I said. "We're here in Barcelona looking for him. He's been missing for over two months."

"And why do you come to me?" she asked. Dona Pretiosa's smile hadn't faded, but it now seemed pasted on, no longer natural.

"Don't you know him?" Pilar asked. "It's important that we find him. His sister felt you might be able to help us."

"I'm afraid I can't." Dona Pretiosa's smile had completely faded. She was speaking now in a soft voice, very slowly, as though weighing each word. "I remember the name," she continued. "He used to come to my cafe many years ago. He was a student then, I think. But I haven't seen him recently."

I sensed that she was lying. "Maria, Pedro's sister, has been killed," I said.

I wanted to shock Dona Pretiosa, and I did. She buried her face in her hands and moaned, "No, poor, poor Pedro!"

"We must find Pedro," Pilar said gently. "We think his life may be in danger. If he has committed no crime, he has no reason to fear us. If he has, giving himself up now might help him."

Dona Pretiosa uncovered her face. Tears now ran down the flat planes of her cheeks. "Pedro has commited no crimes," she said softly. "Why can't you people just leave him alone? Don't you think I know he's in danger?"

"Why do you think he's in danger?" I asked.

Dona Pretiosa didn't answer. She looked away from us toward the folk singer. Tears were still rolling down her face.

"El Grupo Febrero used to meet here," I said. "Would you know how we could get in touch with any of the members other than Pedro?"

Dona Pretiosa turned back to us. "No," she said. "They have all disappeared."

"Within the last two months?"

She nodded.

"So Pedro is with them?"

"No," she said vehemently almost shouting. Then she caught herself. "I mean, I'm not sure where he is, but I don't think he's with the others."

Abruptly she turned away from us. She moved to the coffeebar and began busying herself, wiping the wooden surface of the bar. I followed her.

"Please go away," she said. "You are from the police, no? I already told the men from the police that I don't know where Pedro is. Please leave me alone."

Pilar had followed me to the bar. We exchanged glances. No other police had been sent to talk to Dona Pretiosa. Lorca would have told us.

"When did you speak to these men?" I asked.

"Why, yesterday."

"Look, Dona Pretiosa, those men were not from the police. If they were from the police we would have known about it. You must tell us where Pedro is. If those men do find him, it could be a matter of life and death for him."

"Those men were from El Grupo?"

"Quite possibly."

Dona Pretiosa let out a long moan. "He knew they would find him eventually." She described the three men to us, one very tall, cleanly shaven man, the other two shorter, with dark beards. All of them had been wearing dark business suits.

"Pedro is so afraid of them," she said.

"Why?"

"I cannot tell you. I do not know."

"But you do know where Pedro is?" Pilar asked. "Please tell us. For his sake."

Dona Pretiosa did not speak for many seconds. The only sound in the cafe was the singer's wailing voice. Finally, she cleared her throat, and almost in a whisper said, "He has been hiding in a deserted cottage I own in Felipe, along the coast from the city. He came to me three weeks ago in a panic. He wouldn't tell me why, but eventually I figured out that he was terribly afraid of being caught by members of El Grupo. Once a week I go there and take him food." She then broke down in tears. Pilar took the woman in her arms and comforted her. When she finally ceased crying, Dona Pretiosa gave us directions to the cottage where Pedro was hiding. We promised her we wouldn't hurt him. I only hoped we could keep that promise.

A glorious red and pink sunset accompanied us as we drove along the coastal highway. By the time we reached the village of Felipe the sun had completely set and a full moon had appeared in the sky. Its light shone down on the rocky terrain and showed us a countryside that was almost like a lunar landscape. The village was named after Felipe II, a Spanish king of the sixteenth century, but there was nothing regal about the town. Its rocky stone streets were dotted with small houses made from the same beige stone, and at this hour the streets were almost deserted. Because it was set in from the coastal highway and was perched high above the ocean, it had apparently not been touched by the booming tourist industry that had transformed the surrounding towns. Finally we spotted an old man on one of the streets, walking a mongrel almost as skinny as his master. I stopped the car and asked for directions to the Giralda Place. He pointed us down a rocky road that he said would eventually lead us there.

"You won't find anyone there, though," he said. "The place has been deserted for two years now, ever since Old Man Giralda died."

We explained that we had been sent by Dona Pretiosa, who was Giralda's daughter, and that we were thinking of buying the Giralda cottage.

"Can't imagine what you'd want with it," the old man said, "but I guess it's in demand."

"Why?"

"Some other men were here, earlier this afternoon, looking for the place. I guess Dona Pretiosa has several people looking at the place."

"I guess so," I said. "Too bad we didn't get here first. Thanks."

I steered the Mercedes onto the rocky road the old man had pointed out to us. It was more than

too bad that we hadn't got here first. If the men
who had asked about the place earlier in the day
were from El Grupo, chances are Pedro would already be gone.

The rocky road wound up through steep jagged
mountains and eventually turned to dirt. About
two hundred yards along the dirt road, I pulled the
car to the side of the road.

"We're almost at the top of the hill," I said.
"The cottage can't be far. We'd better walk the rest
of the way." I didn't want Pedro to hear our approach if he was still here, just in case he was
armed or decided to flee.

A coyote called out from the hills as we made
our way up the steep dirt road. After climbing a
couple of dozen yards, we reached the top of the
hill, and the Giraldo cottage came into sight.

"That must be it," Pilar whispered.

The cottage, like the ones in the village of Felipe,
was small and made of beige stone. It stood on the
flat top of the hill, the ground surrounding it bar-
ren except for a couple of low bushes beneath the
front windows. Jagged rock formations edged the
place in a circle.

No light showed from the cottage's windows.
The night air was silent. I was afraid we were too
late.

I touched Pilar's arm, indicating that we should
bear to our left, keeping close to the rock formations that would give us a cover of shadowy
darkness. The rocks were closer to the house's
back, and would afford us more protection if we
went around that way.

"Look," Pilar whispered as we neared the back

of the house. My eyes turned in the direction she indicated. Standing between the back of the house and the rock formation was a black sedan, gleaming in the moonlight. So someone was here still.

As we moved toward the car as a cover, the silence of the night was suddenly punctuated by two gunshots.

Chapter Six

Both Pilar and I froze at the sound of the gunshots. It took us a second to realize that the shots had clearly come from inside the house, and that they hadn't been fired outward, aimed at us. We edged toward the back of the house. From here we could hear voices coming from the windows, and then the sound of a low, guttural laugh. I stood next to the window nearest me. Pilar took up a post at the other window at the back of the house. Because the window was high and narrow, she picked up a metal bucket lying in the yard and stood on it, placing her head against the window.

Up against the window I could see why we'd seen no light coming from the cottage. The windows had been covered with heavy dark cloth from the inside. Even standing right next to them, one could barely see the light that appeared around the windows' edges.

I listened, and my heart gave an extra beat when I realized that the voices were speaking in Russian.

"Now Nozdrev can get the plans," a man's voice said.

"Now that we've got rid of this one," said another man.

"He's supposed to pick up the plans tomorrow?"

"That's what the deal was."

"And then Spain will be in our hands."

At this they both gave a hoarse laugh, then continued talking.

"Too bad this one didn't give us the information we wanted."

At this point I heard a crash to my left. I turned to see Pilar sprawled on the ground, the bucket beside her. The men inside must have also heard her fall, because suddenly all conversation among them stopped. I moved to help Pilar. She was holding her ankle, wincing in pain.

"Damn," she whispered, as I bent down to help her up. "The bucket just gave way beneath me, it must have been rusting."

"Couldn't be helped," I said. I pulled Wilhelmina out of my pocket. Just in time. For at that moment a man of middle height, with a carefully cropped, dark beard, came around the cottage. The gun in his hand was pointed at us. Fortunately his eyes were taking awhile to adjust to the darkness. He squinted toward where we were, then spotted us.

I aimed and fired. The luger's shot echoed loudly against the surrounding rocks. The bullet entered the man's chest as he let out a curse in Russian. Then he fell to the ground, and his gun flew out of his hand and hit the side of the cottage. The man lay motionless, as his blood, now simply a dark shape in the moonlight, flowed onto the light colored ground.

"Are you okay?" I asked Pilar.

She nodded.

"You stay here then and guard the car." She had already taken a Mercury RR8 from her pocket. She hobbled over to the car and crouched behind it.

I rushed around the corner to the front of the house. The primitive wooden door was closed. I kicked at it with all my might until it splintered and opened inward. As I entered the cottage, one of the Russians, another with a shortly cropped beard, came toward me holding a high-powered pistol. He fired at me, but I ducked the shot and his bullet whistled into the empty night air. I aimed Wilhelmina at him, but he came running at me, knocking my aim off track as he shoved into my stomach. I hit him against the side of the head. Blood ran down his face as he staggered backward. He tried to aim his pistol at me again, but my shot was ahead of his. It went straight into his gut, and he slumped against a primitive wooden table, knocking it over.

A lighted kerosene lamp fell from the table igniting a pile of rubbish lying near it. As the kerosene flowed along the floor the leaping flames followed it. There was water in a large pitcher beside the door, which I tipped onto the flames, but to no avail. I started toward a cot in a dark corner of the one-room cottage, hoping to find a blanket. As I approached I realized with a start, that there was a man lying there in the shadows. But he didn't get up off the cot and rush me. He didn't raise a pistol at me. He had two bullets in his head, one through his left eye, the other through his forehead. And he'd been badly beaten by the Russians before they shot him. The side of his head was swollen with a bruise, and there were welts all across his naked back.

I recognized the dead man. I'd seen a picture of him. The large brown eyes, the full lips, the pale skin—like Maria's. I vowed to myself that I'd have my revenge, that I'd find the men responsible for killing Pedro and Maria.

The flames were growning larger now, threatening to engulf the whole corner of the cottage. I picked up a heavy woolen blanket that was on the foot of the cot and threw it on top of the roaring flames. Then I threw my body on top of the blanket. I felt the flame rise up around my face, and tasted the acrid smoke. I rolled across the blanket, then jumping up, I saw that I had managed to put out most of the fire. The flames that still flickered around the edges of the blanket, I stamped out with my feet.

It was then that I heard a volley of gunfire coming from outside. There had been a third Russian in the cabin, who must have escaped through the back and tried to make a getaway in the car. I listened intently. No more shots followed.

Then my heart sank when I heard an engine start up. That meant that Pilar hadn't headed the man off, that she hadn't hit him. He'd hit her. I rushed out the front door just in time to see the sedan pull out from behind the house and head toward the dirt road. I lifted Wilhelmina to fire, but as I sighted the driver's head, a shot rang out and struck the left front tire of the car. Pilar came running to the front of the house, her gun still in her hand, all traces of her limp gone. Thank god. We stood together watching the car, which was now out of control. It missed the turnoff to the dirt road and careened into the large rock formation with an ear-splitting crash.

"He got past me," Pilar explained, "but then I aimed again."

"And hit. Good work."

We went to the totalled car, and what we saw wasn't a pretty sight. The driver's head had gone through the windshield, and was now a bloody pulp with glass shards sticking out from the skin. From the way his body was twisted against the steering wheel, it was clear that the man's back was broken and that he was dead.

"His name is Mihail Brodsky," Pilar said. "I recognized him immediately. He's one of Moscow's top agents in Spain, and is particularly noted for his work as an assassin. And he also, although you couldn't tell it by looking at him now, fits the description Dona Pretiosa gave of one of the men who came into her cafe."

"The other two fit her descriptions, also," I said. I lifted Brodsky's body out of the car and went through his pockets. I found nothing.

"Nick," Pilar said, as we walked back toward the house, "they were talking about the nuclear plans, weren't they?"

"It sounded like it all right. And Nozdrev's supposed to get hold of them tomorrow. It looks like El Grupo and the Russians are playing nuclear footsie."

"Yes," Pilar said, "it's a grim business." She seemed terribly depressed.

"You sure you're all right Pilar? Your foot?"

"I'll be fine."

"We'd better check out the other two."

Pilar went to the man outside, while I headed back to the cabin to check out the man I'd gunned down there. This was a grim business, as Pilar said. We'd had all of our worst fears confirmed tonight. One: El Grupo *did* know that what they had in their hands were diagrams and instructions for nuclear weapons. Two: El Grupo and the Russians were playing ball. And three: the Russians were getting the nuclear plans tomorrow and unless we stopped them, the two groups would, "take control of this country," as Brodsky had so succinctly put it.

The first time I searched the man in the cottage I didn't find anything on him. The second time, however, I discovered a folded slip of paper in the bottom of his back trouser pocket. Written on the paper was a phone number, with the initial "N" written beneath it.

"I found nothing," Pilar said as she entered the cottage. "What about you?"

I showed her the slip of paper.

"It's a Barcelona number," she said. "I recognize the prefix. Do you think N stands for Nozdrev?"

"I certainly hope so." Then I motioned Pilar toward the cot in the corner. Pilar stood looking down at the figure on the cot.

"Pedro?"

I nodded. Why had the Russians wanted to beat and then murder him? What information did he have that they wanted? And if the Russians were connected with El Grupo, what did that mean about Pedro's connections with El Grupo? Were

there one or two branches of El Grupo? Still there
were no answers.

I was silent during most of the drive back to Barcelona, thinking about Maria and Pedro. I couldn't
get the images of their large dark eyes out of my
mind. Their murders seemed to be totally senseless
in this wretched game between terrorist power bro-
kers. Sadly, the lives of lots of "little people" like
Maria and Pedro get caught up and demolished in
these big international struggles.

Pilar must have sensed my mood, because she
was pretty silent herself for most of the trip. Maybe
she was thinking some of the same thoughts I was.
Eventually she spoke.

"Nick, Lorca told me about you and Maria. Are
you thinking of her?"

I nodded.

"I'm so sorry," she said, placing her hand on my
shoulder.

"Thanks. I'll bear up. It's all part of the game."

"One always does, bear up, doesn't one?" she
said sadly. Then there was nothing more to say.
But she left her hand on my shoulder, and it felt
good there.

Back in my hotel room in Barcelona, I got out a
scrambling device, just in case anyone should be
listening in, and we placed a call to Lorca. I gave
him a brief outline of the night's events, and he said
he'd sent an ambulance to pick up the bodies, and
a tow car for the sedan. Then I gave him the
bombshell about the nuclear plans that Nozdrev
was to pick up tomorrow. He whistled into the receiver.

"Christ, Nick, this is bad. As bad as it can get. We've got to head Nozdrev off. I'll put my men on the phone number and get back to you as soon as possible. Don't either of you leave the hotel. Stay put. I want you there and ready to leave as soon as we locate an address for that number. Let's just hope it is Nozdrev's number. If we don't intercept those plans before the Russians we're going to have a major international crisis on our hands. I'll also send out sketches of Nozdrev to every police station in the country. Now, I'll talk to you later."

"We'll be here," I said and hung up. "Well," I said, turning to Pilar, "looks like we're staying in for the rest of the night."

"Waiting for Nozdrev?"

"Waiting for Nozdrev. Could be a long wait."

"Well Nick, what shall we do while we wait?" She had that teasing note in her voice I'd noticed the first night at her party. Also, I couldn't help but notice that she had kicked off her shoes and had stretched out on my bed while I talked to Lorca on the phone. My eyes moved from the golden helmet of her hair against the pillow to the nipples thrusting out of the light clinging tanktop. Then I looked into her pale, beautiful face. She returned my gaze.

"I'm much too excited to go back to my bedroom to sleep," she said. Her low, sexy voice was again teasing.

"Good," I said. "I'm excited too."

Then Pilar stretched out her arms, beckoning me to join her on the bed, and I moved into her arms. I thrust my body on top of hers, clothes and all, and I felt her arms greedily encircling my back.

"I've wanted you ever since that first night at my party," Pilar said.

"And I've wanted you."

Our lips and our tongues met in a long, long kiss. Then I raised myself up. As I straddled Pilar, I removed her tank top and her skirt and panties. I threw off my own clothes and bent back down to her. Supporting myself on my elbows, I kissed and licked her full, smooth breasts. Her rosy nipples became erect under the probing of my tongue. As her hand caressed my hair and the back of my neck, I slid my own hand down and touched the rich moistness below.

"Oh, please Nick," Pilar whispered.

I moved my body into hers very slowly, and she let out a long, low sigh of pleasure. Her hands played on my back, her long fingernails tapping out a musical rhythmn to accompany my own thrusts. I gradually increased my speed and felt Pilar change her own rhythm in response. Her hands now caressed my shoulders, my back, my buttocks. Her legs parted wider and she thrust them over my back, as though she wanted me as deeply inside of her as possible. I pressed further and harder. Pilar began moaning, softly at first, and then louder and wilder, until finally we climaxed together, perfectly, and she was still.

We both lay motionless for many seconds. Then Pilar reached out and touched my cheek.

"You were even more wonderful than I expected," she said. The feeling was certainly mutual. More than satisfied, we both drifted off into sleep.

I awakened with a start to the loud ringing of the telephone. As I reached for the receiver, I noted the clock beside the bed. It read 4:30 a.m.

"Hello?"

"Nick, Lorca here. My research department has located the address that corresponds to that phone number you found. It's in a residential district in the northern part of the city. I've already sent some men to keep watch on the house while you and Pilar get there—just in case Nozdrev's there and decides to go out."

Lorca told me his men would be in a gray coupe and gave me their license number so I could identify them. I asked him if he had any new information about the case.

"No new communiques from El Grupo," he said. "But I did get some news on those men you shot down two days ago at Maria's. All of them *had* been in the Spanish army. Strangely, though, they all have very distinguished records, all of them performed extremely well. There was not a single dishonorable discharge among them. Anyway, my men are now trying to locate their relatives and see if we can come up with anything from that angle.

"Listen, Nick," Lorca continued, "the important thing now is to stop Nozdrev, if he is at that house. But I also want you to try to take him alive if at all possible. He'd be more useful to us that way. We might be able to get some information out of him about El Grupo. But do what you have to do. Good luck."

I hung up. Pilar was looking at me, her green eyes clouded over with sleep. I told her to rise and shine and relayed what information Lorca had given me. Pilar rose, and as the sheets fell from her, I had to check my impulse to reach out and encircle that gorgeous statuesque body. There was no time for all that now.

It was still dark outside when we arrived at the address Lorca had given us. We parked the car around the corner and then headed toward the small wooden house. The place was bordered by a small, stone garden wall, but the front door was in clear sight of the street. I spotted the small, gray coupe across the street and went over to look at its license plates. They checked out, and as I moved to the car's front door, the driver rolled down the window.

"Mr. Bryan?" he said.

"Yes. Anything happening here?"

"Not since we arrived. No one's entered or left the house since four-fifteen."

"Is there a back entrance?"

"Yeah, we've got a couple of men round back watching it." The driver checked with the men in back via his two-way radio just to make sure nothing new had developed in the last few minutes. Nothing had.

"Okay," I said. "Stay here and signal us if anyone approaches the house."

I decided our best bet was to enter the house through the back door. Pilar and I stepped over the low fence into the garden and circled around to the back. The house was dark and silent. I looked through a back window into a small, modern kitchen. An adjustable key inserted easily into the back door. After I jiggled the key for a few seconds, the tumbler clicked and the door opened inward.

I unpocketed Wilhelmina and stepped inside. Pilar, gun in hand, followed me. The kitchen led into a small hall, off of which we found a dining room and living room. Both were dark and empty.

From the living room another hall led to what were apparently two bedrooms. The door of one of these rooms was open and we checked it out: also empty. The door to the second bedroom, however, was closed.

If Nozdrev was asleep in the house, that was the room he was in. I asked Pilar for her high-powered flashlight. If Nozdrev was asleep, I planned to surprise him with the light in his eyes before he had a chance to respond. I slowly turned the knob of the bedroom door. The door creaked slightly as it opened inward. I suddenly shined the light into Nozdrev's face. Or what should have been his face. What the beams illuminated was a pillow and an empty bed. A spread covered the bed, and it looked as though no one had been sleeping here tonight.

We returned to the living room and started searching the place to see if we could come up with any information that might tell us whether or not this house was indeed Nozdrev's headquarters. If he was staying here, there might be some information in the house about his meeting with El Grupo today. The living room was decorated with standard modern furniture and was entirely nondescript. Even the abstract paintings on the wall looked like they had been sold by lot, and the whole place was devoid of any traces of personal tastes or eccentricities. A typical safehouse set-up.

While Pilar checked out the walls for bugging, I went through the drawers of cabinets and tables here and in the dining room. They were as empty and spotless as in a newly-cleaned hotel room. Pilar concluded that the place wasn't bugged.

The kitchen seemed as empty of personal traces

and as nondescript as the living and dining rooms. In one of the cabinets, however, Pilar found a half-filled bottle of extremely expensive Russian vodka. The first indication that whoever was living here had to be Russian was that the vodka wasn't a brand that was imported to Spain.

The second bedroom offered us no further clues. In the master bedroom all the drawers and bureaus were empty, as were the cabinets in the bathroom. In the closet in the hall, though, I found two newly-cleaned suits, still in their cellophane protectors. Ripping off the cellophane I discovered that the suits were made by an English tailor on Bond Street. He was a tailor whom I knew many high Russian officials favored. And the dimensions of the suits confirmed for me that this was indeed Nozdrev's hideaway. Nozdrev was exactly six feet, five and a half inches tall, with an extremely broad barrel chest, and an exceptionally small waist. There weren't many men besides Nozdrev who could fit into these jackets and pants.

So this was where Nozdrev stayed. But where was he now?

At this point we could only wait here and hope that Nozdrev returned. In the meantime, we decided to go over the entire house again in the hope that we might find some further clues to the Russian's activities. We searched the living room and dining room and kitchen even more thoroughly than before. We checked the molding and the window frames, looked behind the paintings for a safe, took all the cushions off the sofas and chairs. We found nothing.

We went over the bedrooms again with a fine-toothed comb and again turned up nothing. It was discouraging. I had almost given up when I picked up a message pad from beside the telephone in the master bedroom. I had flipped through it before and all of its pages were blank. Touching it now I felt a slight indentation beneath my fingers. I picked up a pencil and began lightly running it across the top sheet of paper. Sure enough, letters and numbers began to appear on the pad. The indentation came from a message written on the sheet of paper above this one. When I had covered the entire sheet in gray, a message stood out in white. It read: "El Sol #32-A, 12th, noon."

Excited, I showed the message to Pilar. Today was the twelfth, so it was clear that Nozdrev was meeting someone at noon, quite possibly the men from El Grupo. But where? What was "El Sol?" "Sol" was the Spanish word for sun, but what did it mean here? A restaurant, perhaps? A club? A gymnasium?

"We've got to find out what 'Sol' is," I said to Pilar. We got out Nozdrev's telephone books and combed through them. Not a single listing for anything in Barcelona called "El Sol." I took a miniature, computerized telephone from my pocket that Lorca had given me. I dialed him.

I explained to him that Nozdrev wasn't here, but that I was certain this was his hideaway. I gave Lorca the message I'd found by the phone, and he promised to put his research department on it and see if they could come up with the meaning of "El Sol." He advised Pilar and me to sit tight in the meantime—in case Nozdrev came back to his house between now and noon. There wasn't much else we could do.

As I put the computer phone back in my pocket,

I realized that the sun had risen. I checked my watch: 8 a.m. Only four hours before the meeting of the Russians and El Grupo and possibly the beginning of Doomsday. It made me shudder.

By 11:15, I was convinced that Nozdrev wasn't coming back here before his noon meeting. I was just taking out the computer phone to ring up Lorca and tell him that Pilar and I might as well leave when Lorca buzzed me. He said that the only thing his men had been able to come up with was that there was a beach to the south of Barcelona that was sometimes called "El Sol." It was a long shot, just a guess that the "Sol" on the slip of paper I'd found was this beach, but at the moment it was the only guess we had. The #32-A could refer to a cabana number. Lorca explained that El Sol was the third public beach after we hit the coastal highway south of the city.

"Can you make it there by noon?"

"We'll do the best we can."

Chapter Seven

Barcelona pedestrians are notorious for crossing in front of cars, and it seemed as though every few yards or so I had to slam on my brakes and come to a screeching halt to avoid running down women loaded with shopping bags and smartassed teenagers strolling nonchalantly across the streets.

As we neared the center of the city the noonday traffic became more and more dense. The air was filled with the smell of gasoline exhaust and the sounds of irate drivers honking and shouting at one another. By the time we reached the Federal Plaza at the end of the Ramblas, we were in the middle of a real traffic jam. A car had stalled and was creating a gigantic traffic snarl ahead of us; cars moved only at a snail's pace.

I checked my watch. It was 11:30 already. We were in the far right-hand lane of the crowded six-lane intersection. Honking the horn, I steered the Mercedes onto the wide sidewalk to my right. Pedestrians fled before me in panic, shouting curses, and two traffic cops in the middle of the street blew their shrill whistles and gestured angrily at me. But I stepped on the gas and kept making my way down the sidewalk. Glancing in the rearview mirror I saw that I'd started something. Other cars were now pulling onto the sidewalk behind me, and soon this would be just another lane of traffic, as slow-moving as the rest. But fortunately I was well ahead of the cars behind me, and had already made it around the intersection and pulled back into the street. A few blocks more, and we reached the entrance to the coastal highway and headed south.

The traffic was less dense on the highway, and I quickly managed to pick up speed and miles. We drove alongside the glistening, aquamarine ocean. Gradually the larger buildings on the edge of the city gave way to smaller ones, and soon the land was pure, sandy coastline, dotted only occasionally by a house or inn. The first public beach came into view, then several miles further down the coast a second beach appeared.

"It will be the next beach," Pilar said excitedly.

After a stretch of several more miles of sand and water, El Sol came into view. It nestled along the white sand between the ocean and the highway. A long line of cars was parked on the side of the highway, and looking down I could see that El Sol was packed. I could also see that the place had a large complex of cabanas.

Twelve noon exactly. No time to waste. We parked and hurriedly descended the steep steps leading down to the beach. At the foot of the stairs was a big white bathhouse, whose large front window was open.

"Can I help you?" said a deeply tanned young stud, who was leaning out of the bathhouse window.

"We'd like a cabana," I said. "Has anyone

checked into number thirty-two-A?"

"Let me check," he said, moving toward the back wall of the building where the keys to the cabanas were kept. "Not many people request specific cabanas. You been here before?" he asked.

"No."

"Didn't think so. You from the city?" His question was directed at Pilar, who he'd been eyeing since we arrived. He wanted to strike up a conversation with her, but his slow, lazy speech and movements were infuriating under the circumstances.

"My husband and I are supposed to meet a friend who said he'd be in cabana thirty-two-A. We just wanted to check and see whether or not he's arrived yet."

The beachbum turned back to the rows of keys. "Looks like you're in luck," he drawled. "Someone's already taken thirty-two-A."

"Which way is it?"

The man came back to the window and pointed toward a wooden path through the cabanas. "You take that passageway, then take a left, and then another left at the end of that passageway. Thirty-two-A will be the third cabana from the end of that section."

We took off in a run.

"Hey," the stud cried indignantly after us. "I thought you wanted a cabana for yourself!"

The large complex of cabanas was a wooden structure set a foot or so above the sand. Its layout was like a maze so we followed the directions the young stud had given us to the letter. The place was crowded with men, women, and children parading in their bathing suits along the open air wooden passageways. As we took the final turn, we passed three men who looked strangely out of place among the other half-naked people here. The three were wearing jeans and work shirts. Glancing down at my own suit, I laughed. I supposed Pilar and I looked pretty out of place here too.

At thirty-A we slowed our pace. I unpocketed Wilhelmina, although I kept my gun hand under my jacket so I wouldn't alarm the bathers passing by. Pilar took out her pistol also, keeping it behind her purse. The white louvered shutters of thirty-two-A were drawn tightly shut, and the cabana's door was closed. I motioned to Pilar and she flattened herself against the outside wall of the cabana, beside the door. Then I kicked open the white wooden door and brought Wilhelmina out from under my jacket as I entered the room. The blinding, white sunlight streamed into the cabana and illuminated Nozdrev.

"If you want to live," I said, "don't move." I waved my gun as he moved his hand toward his chest. His hand retreated. Again he moved his hand toward his chest, but he didn't complete the gesture.

Then I noticed the spot of red near the shoulder of his white terrycloth beach robe. I reached down and jerked open the robe. Nozdrev's eyes looked into mine, but he didn't move. His large, muscular body was naked beneath the robe, except for a pair of swimming briefs. The spot of red on his robe had come from a knife wound on the left side of his chest, just below the armpit. Another knife wound, an enormous gash, was just below his rib cage.

Blood from this second wound ran down his stomach, over his crotch, and was forming a pool of red on the white tile floor of the cabana.

"Help me," he gasped. Then it hit me. The men in the blue jeans and work shirts we'd passed! Of course! El Grupo!

I called to Pilar and told her to run after the men we'd seen and try to prevent them from leaving the beach. I'd join her as soon as I was through with Nozdrev. He didn't have long to live, and I wanted to try to get as much information as I could out of him before he drew his last breath.

"Help me," the big Russian said, as I turned back to him. His voice was weak and there were large beads of sweat on his forehead and chest.

"All right," I said. "I'll help you, but I want some information in exchange."

"Get me to a doctor," he gasped.

"I will when you tell me what you're doing here." Nozdrev was silent for a number of seconds. He must have been struggling between his sense of duty and his desire to live. Finally, he spoke.

"I was here to meet some of my men. Some lunatic broke in and attacked me."

"You can do better than that Nozdrev. The truth. Now. Do you want me to get you to a doctor or don't you?"

"El Grupo," Nozdrev said in a very faint voice.

"Why were you meeting them here?"

There was another period of silence. Nozdrev's gaze moved down his torso to the pool of blood at his feet. Then his eyes returned to mine.

"You'll get me to a hospital if I tell you?" he asked. "And I must have asylum with the Americans. Can you offer me asylum if I confess, Nick Carter?" So he knew who I was. Nozdrev was desperate now, and I assured him that I'd get him to a hospital and that the American government would do all it could to protect him from the KGB. But I knew he wouldn't live long enough for either a hospital or the U.S. government to do him any good.

"El Grupo has stolen nuclear plans from Spain." His voice was almost a whisper now. I had to bend down and place my ear next to his mouth. I felt his panting breath against my face.

"Have the Russians been working with El Grupo all along?"

"No. Only recently. They proposed to share the plans with us as part of a favor."

"What was the favor?"

"To hunt down and kill an enemy of theirs."

"Pedro Salas?"

"Yes. But El Grupo tricked me. We killed him, like they wanted and then . . . they . . . came . . . here . . . today . . . and . . . tried . . . tried . . . to . . . murder . . . me." Nozdrev's words came slowly now, with a great deal of difficulty. He had only a few seconds left. I almost pitied him.

"Why did they want Pedro Salas dead?"

"He . . . was . . . an . . . enemy."

"What had he done to El Grupo?"

"He . . . was . . . trying . . . " Suddenly I felt no more breath against my face. Nozdrev's eyes stared straight ahead. I took his wrist between my fingers: the pulse was gone.

I closed his eyes and drew the terrycloth robe back across his body, then left the cabana, closing the door behind me. On the boardwalk, the sun worshippers and pleasure seekers offered a sharp contrast to the scene I'd just taken part in. Two young boys chased a third down the passageway. The boy being chased was wearing a dimestore Indian headband, and the other two were yelling, "Bang, Bang, you're dead," as they went after him. Pilar and the men from El Grupo were nowhere in sight. .

I headed down the passageway, toward the exit. Then a gunshot rang out. It seemed to come from another part of the cabana complex, closer to the ocean than where I was.

"Pilar," I yelled and headed in that direction.

"Here," she answered, and I tried to make my way through the maze of passageways to reach her. I heard another gunshot. People stared at me as I ran past them, and all along the passageways heads began bopping out of cabana windows. I suddenly found myself in a dead-end passageway.

"Pilar," I yelled again.

"Nick!" Her voice was near. I could tell that she was in a passageway parallel to the one I was in. I ran to the end of this passageway and whipped around the corner. Pilar came running toward me.

"Quick, to the beach," she said. As we ran she explained that she'd followed the three men we'd seen back to a cabana they'd apparently rented. When they'd tried to leave the cabana, she'd shot at the door, hoping to keep them trapped inside until I arrived. But they'd shot at her through the window, and as she scurried to take cover, they'd run out. She'd hit one man as he headed toward the beach, but the other two had been too quick for her.

When we reached the beach, I could see the two men in the distance. They were clever: they'd deliberately headed for the most crowded part of the beach. Their blue work shirts weaved in and out of the throng. If we shot at them now, we'd risk hitting innocent bystanders.

Already the gunshots from the cabanas had created pandemonium on the beach. Mothers were screaming for their children. Swimmers had come out of the water and were standing along the shore. People who had been moving about the beach had flattened themselves on the ground, while others who had been spread out sunning themselves had risen. No one seemed to know what position to take in order to avoid the gunshots that they thought might be fired at them.

One of the El Grupo men veered away from his companion and ran toward the beach's entrance. I told Pilar to bear left and head him off at the steps while I continued after the man whose blue shirt was still bobbing in and out of the crowd. Before long, though, the man had passed beyond the groups of people and was running along an empty stretch of beach. He was in shooting range and a fairly easy target, but I wanted to take him alive. I had to give him credit: He was an Olympic caliber runner. I kept pace with him, but I didn't gain on him until he began nearing a cliff which jutted out abruptly into the water, interrupting the shoreline. The man slowed his pace and looked around, deciding what to do. He had three choices. He could turn around and head back toward me, he could go into the ocean, or he could climb over the cliff to the other side of the beach. He chose the latter.

By the time I reached the cliff, he'd already scurried halfway up it. I started climbing after him. Looking up, I saw that he'd stopped on a ledge of rock and was taking a pistol out of his work shirt. I raised my luger. He fired first, and narrowly missed my head. I fired back, aiming at his gun. His pistol jerked out of his hand and he himself tottered backward, unbalanced by the impact of my bullet. For a moment he hung precariously to the side of the cliff. But then he regained his footing and continued up the sharp white rocks. The cliff wasn't high and soon he disappeared over its edge.

As I reached the top I peered cautiously over the side. The man in the blue shirt was nowhere in sight. I figured he must have already scurried across the cliff's top and begun his descent to the other side of the beach. I rushed to the opposite side of the cliff.

I felt a crushing blow against the back of my head. I staggered and went down, my face against the rocks. The man must have hidden behind a boulder and come up on me from behind. It felt like he'd hit me with a heavy stone. I lay on my stomach, dazed and motionless. He must have figured I was out cold, for I heard him approach and bend down toward me. I felt his hand against my own as he tried to extract the luger from my fingers. I summoned all my strength and leaped to my feet. He cried out in surprise.

Our hands, his left, my right, were gripping each other and the luger. I saw this member of El Grupo clearly for the first time. He was tanned and handsome and in his late twenties. A lock of his long hair hung over his forehead, and there was a small black mustache above his thick, surly lips. He snarled at me, revealing jagged, but very white teeth. The pressure of his thick hand against my own was like a vise. I drew back my free fist and moved it toward his gut, just as he drew back his free fist and aimed at my chin. We both hit on target. He doubled over, and I staggered backwards from the force of his knuckles. The gun fell to the ground. He leaped for it, but I managed to kick the gun away just as his hand reached out for it. It flew over the cliff and banged against the rocks below. From the distance I could hear the sound of more gunshots and in the far distance the moan of a police siren.

I stood facing my antagonist. We were now on the far edge of the cliff, overhanging the ocean. My back was toward the ocean, and he made a run at me. His hands were straight out in front of him; he meant to push me over the cliff. It would have been easy enough for me to dodge him and let his speed send *him* over the edge. But I didn't want to get rid of him that way. If he went off, he'd either drown or swim away. In either case, I'd have lost my chance to question him. So I braced myself for his blow, rooting my strength as firmly to the ground as I could. He rammed into me, and I grabbed him, clinging as tightly as I could to his back. But I'd miscalculated either the angle of his approach or his speed. I lurched backward as he hit and we both went flying over the side of the cliff.

Our grips on one another released as we sailed through the air and plunged into the water. I felt myself going deep down into the ocean's icy depths. Eventually the descent ended, and, holding my breath, I sprang myself to the ocean's surface. I looked around. The surface of the water was empty. Then I saw the man's head bob up. When he saw me, he swan toward me and immediately grabbed at my throat. His grip around my neck forced my head under water, but I was able to pull him under water, too. We struggled in an underwater stalemate for many minutes. There was no question of bringing him in alive now. It was him or me, all a question of who could hold out for air the longest. Suddenly his face contorted, his eyes bugged out like a fish's, and his hands slipped away from my shoulders. He thrashed and his mouth gulped frantically for air. But what he got was water. I didn't loosen my grip on him. Finally he quit thrashing.

My lungs felt like they were going to burst when I finally took in some air, but I managed to swim back to shore. Looking back, I saw that the blue-shirted body had risen to the surface and was now being battered against the cliff by the waves. I walked back along the empty sand to the crowded part of the beach. Police cars and an ambulance, their lights flashing, had already arrived on the scene. A crowd formed around two ambulance attandents as they carried two men in blue work shirts away on stretchers.

Pilar looked at me anxiously. "Are you all right Nick?"

"I'll be okay. What happened to you?"

"I'm afraid I had to shoot the second man to keep him from getting away."

"Yeah, I had to kill my man too. It's tough."

As we made our way through the staring crowd, someone handed me a blanket, which I draped around my shoulders. We stopped at the ambulance and I spoke to the driver:

"You'd better send your men to Cabana thirty-two-A. You'll find another corpse there."

Chapter Eight

I didn't know what to make of this new wrinkle in the affair of El Grupo. I assumed that Nozdrev hadn't been lying about his dealings with El Grupo. I've been around lots of dying men, and I can usually figure out their psychology pretty well. From what I'd seen it looked like Nozdrev was too desperate and too near death to make up the incredible story he'd told me. But why had El Grupo tricked the Russians and then killed Nozdrev?

It had crossed my mind before that there might be two branches of El Grupo, and in this context the murder of Nozdrev made some sense. I speculated that one of the branches of El Grupo, the branch that had kidnapped Rodriguez and that had the nuclear weapons plan, had gotten in touch with Nozdrev. In exchange for sharing the nuclear weapons plans, they'd convinced the Russians to find and knock off Pedro, who was a member of the rival branch of El Grupo. When Pedro's branch found out about his death, they had killed the Russian in retaliation.

This theory, though, had a lot of loopholes. First, if Nozdrev had been playing ball with one branch of El Grupo, why had he set up a meeting with the second group? It didn't make sense. An even more serious objection to the two-group theory was that there was no concrete evidence that Pedro had been working with anyone. From what Dona Pretiosa had told us, it sounded like Pedro had been pretty much in isolation, at least for the last three weeks. He seemed to be hiding out, alone, from El Grupo. This led to another question. If Pedro was an "enemy" of his former comrades, why hadn't he come to the police with information about them? By the same token, if there *were* two El Grupos, one "good," one "bad," why hadn't the good group come forward?

The deeper one became immersed in the case, the more confusing and complicated it became. The only good thing about the newest twist was that the Russians probably wouldn't be playing ball with El Grupo anymore. Not after they'd been double-crossed and had their man killed. It was even possible now that the Russians might help us track down the people behind Nozdrev's murder.

If El Grupo's betrayal of the Russians was re-assuring in this sense, it was frightening in another. If the Spaniards were crazy enough to risk the wrath of one of the two most powerful defense and espionage forces on earth, there was no telling what they'd come up with next. It seemed likely that El Grupo wasn't just playing an ordinary game of power politics. Power politics can get pretty vicious, but it's seldom irrational. El Grupo did seem irrational, and it wasn't hard to imagine something as mad as international nuclear blackmail in their future.

Pilar and I discussed all this as we drove back

from the beach to the center of Barcelona. We decided our best bet at this point was for one of us to return and question Dona Pretiosa some more. She had seemed to care about Pedro, and she also seemed to have been pretty tight at one point with some other members of El Grupo. Perhaps when she found out what his former comrades had done to Pedro, she'd be willing to give us their names.

When we returned to our luxury hotel, I left Pilar at the door of her room next to mine and went to change out of my still wet clothes. When I stepped into my room, I got a shock. The place had been completely ransacked, turned upside down. The mattress was on the floor, its fluffy white stuffing spilling out. Someone had done a job on it with a knife. All the room's drawers had been turned upside down. The architectural drawings I'd brought from Madrid were ripped, fragments of them scattered about the floor. My suitcases were open, their linings also slashed by a knife. My jackets, pants, and shirts lay in a pile at the front of the closet, their pockets turned out. A Nikon I'd brought to make slides was smashed. There was another mess in the bathroom. Bottles lay shattered on the floor; after-shave lotion oozed out across the tile. Even my razor had been taken apart (to see if it had a hidden microphone in it?).

A knock came from the door to my suite. I unpocketed Wilhelmina for the umpteenth time today and moved back into the bedroom.

"Who is it?" I yelled, making my way toward the door.

"Pilar." I put Wilhelmina away and let Pilar in.

She looked around at the chaos.

"You, too?" she said. She told me her room had also been totally torn apart. "They even cut up the cups of two of my brassieres, I guess to see if they had hidden microphones in them or something."

I laughed. Naturally whoever had searched our rooms hadn't found anything that could have done them any good. We were both too careful to leave anything around that suggested our connection with the El Grupo case or our secret identities as agents.

"I don't think it was the Russians," Pilar said.

"No, it's not their style. If they wanted to search our rooms, they'd have been discreet."

"El Grupo?" Pilar suggested.

"Perhaps. It looks to me like someone's trying to scare us. Whoever did this may or may not have been looking for something in particular, but you can be damned sure they wanted to let us know that they were here."

"And that they want us to lay off."

"Precisely."

Pilar was thoughtful. "They went through both our rooms, Nick. That means they know we're working together." It did indeed mean just that. I decided it would probably be a good idea if we split up for awhile. We'd each find a separate place to stay, places that would be less conspicuous than the big hotel where we were now. I thought it would be a good idea for me to camp out in some cheap hotel, one of those obscure pensions on the little streets off the old section of the Ramblas. Pilar suggested that she stay with her friend Juan, known to me as El Conde Ruiz.

She explained: "He's in residence here in his large estate on the outskirts of town. I told him at my party that I was coming to Barcelona for a few days to check out the new shows at the galleries, and he invited me then to stay with him."

I looked at Pilar, her fine breasts, the golden hair, the rosy face, those dazzling pale green eyes—everything about her that turned me on. And I remembered El Conde Ruiz's handsome face from her party and the intimate tones of their voices as they'd spoken together and the knowing looks they'd exchanged. I surprised myself by feeling a sharp twinge of jealousy. Personally I didn't like the idea of Pilar staying at Ruiz's, but professionally I couldn't come up with any objection to it. Pilar's "cover," after all, was her real identity as a wealthy society lady and patron of the arts, so it was a good idea that she slip back into that identity and visit someone of her own set. Besides, El Conde Ruiz was one of the wealthiest men in Spain, and his secluded estate was well guarded. Pilar would be safe there.

While Pilar went back to her room to phone El Conde Ruiz, I placed a call to Lorca.

"Good work, Nick," he greeted me. "I've already heard from the Barcelona police about what happened at El Sol this afternoon. I can't help wishing, though, that you'd been able to take either Nozdrev or one of El Grupo's men alive. Do you have the nuclear plans?"

"I wish I'd taken someone alive too, Lorca. And no, I don't have the nuclear plans." I outlined for him what had really happened at the beach. Lorca was as puzzled by El Grupo's killing of Nozdrev as

I was. He said he'd try to go through diplomatic channels and set up an appointment with the Russian ambassador. Now that El Grupo had apparently turned on their men, the Russians might be willing to cooperate with us. Of course, the embassy would never officially admit that they even had secret agents in Spain. But if they could be convinced that El Grupo was working against everyone's best interests, they might give us some "background information" (that is, whatever they knew) about the Spaniards who had killed Nozdrev.

Lorca also relayed the sad news that it looked like El Grupo had struck again. A bomb in Talavera de la Reina, near Toledo, had gone off this afternoon in a post office, killing over a dozen postal workers and citizens. The killings bore the mark of El Grupo, and Lorca felt that there would no doubt be a new communique about the incident from El Grupo tonight. He'd ordered every local police chief to place at least two men at every radio and t.v. station and at every newspaper in the country. That way, he hoped he could catch one of El Grupo's delivery men when he brought the latest tape. The group was becoming more and more brazen, and Lorca was making an all out effort to capture at least one member of their team.

After Lorca had rung off, I started packing. Pilar returned to the room.

"It's all set," she said. "Juan is delighted I'm coming. He's been trying to get me to visit him here for ages. I told him I'd been here a couple of days and was tired of staying at the hotel. He's sending his chauffeur for me. I think he was a little miffed that I hadn't come to him in the first place."

I bet he was. And I hated to see her go. I took
her in my arms and our mouths met in a long, reluctant goodbye.

I left the Mercedes and most of my luggage in a
large parking garage near our hotel. Then I hailed
a cab and had the driver drop me at the less af-
fluent section to the west of the Ramblas. With
only a small suitcase in hand, I wandered on foot
past the small shops, the bars, and apartment
dwellings. It didn't take me long to find what I was
after. From a second story window above a pastry
shop, I saw a sign that read, "Rooms for Rent, 2
pesatas per night." That was the equivalent of
about three and a half dollars in American money.
I rang a bell beside a door on the ground floor.

"Yes?" The head of an enormously fat woman
appeared in the window next to the sign.

"Any rooms available?" I called up to her. The
big head disappeared, and after a rather long wait
I was buzzed through the wrought-iron door. At
the top of a flight of narrow stairs, the woman
whose head I'd seen, greeted me. She must have
weighed three hundred pounds.

"How long will you be staying?" she asked me. I
told her a week. "We clean and change the sheets
only once a week, and you'll have to give me a
week's money in advance," she said. I gave her the
money, and after I'd signed the register in an alias,
she led me up another narrow flight of stairs. She
waddled in front of me, and it was slow going, because of her bulk. At the top, she paused, panting
for breath.

"The shower is to the left there," she said, indicating a door in the dimly-lit hallway. "You pay

twenty-five pesetas if you want the hot water turned on. Let me know an hour before you need it. To the right there is the toilet."

The room she took me to was at the end of the hall. She opened the door and handed me two keys.

"This other key is for the door downstairs. Be sure and close it tightly behind you when you go out and come in. I run a safe place here."

After she'd left, I surveyed the room. The walls were dark green, the floor was of colorless linoleum. It was a front room with a small, shuttered window looking down onto the streets I'd just come up from. The only pieces of furniture were a big, old-fashioned double bed, and a well-worn lounge chair near the window. The "closet" was a metal rack in a corner near the door. The place certainly wasn't luxurious, but it was exactly the kind of place I wanted at the moment. No one would think of looking for me here.

I called Pilar a block from my new lodgings and told her what I was up to for the evening. We agreed to meet at my pension the next morning. Then I hailed a cab. By the time I reached the Barrio Chino the sun had set. The place was even more garish and decadent at night than in the daytime. Blinking tubes of neon, spelling out the names of bars, cast a rainbow of color on the strolling crowds. As I got out of the taxi a dark-skinned woman, with bright red hair, and skin-tight gold pants approached me.

"I have a nice treat for you honey," she said, as she took my arm.

"I'm sure you do," I said, shaking off her arm,

"but I don't have time now." She cursed me briefly, but then moved away and took up her station again by a lamp post.

Dona Pretiosa's coffeehouse was crowded this time. The folksinger was male, with long hair and pale skin. His audience was made up of boys who looked pretty much like him and young girls in peasant blouses and jeans. I saw Dona Pretiosa standing at the expresso bar toward the back of the room. She nodded and motioned me to come to her. Her eyes were questioning and tiny lines of anxiety formed around her mouth as she greeted me.

"I hope you kept your promise," she said, "and did not harm Pedro."

"I kept my promise. I didn't harm him. Others did."

"Others?"

"The men who came to see you yesterday afternoon reached Pedro before we did. I'm afraid he's dead."

The cup Dona Pretiosa was holding clattered to the floor, and she grabbed at the bar to support herself. I stepped behind the bar and put my arm around the distraught woman. I asked a waitress standing nearby to take over for a while, and I guided Dona Pretiosa to an empty table at the back of the coffeehouse. As she cried softly, I waited. I didn't want to press her too soon.

Finally she looked up at me. Her eyes were still brimming with tears. She spoke a single word. "How?"

"They shot him." The singer had ended his song and the people in the front of the cafe cheered and applauded him enthusiastically. I grimaced at the inadvertent irony of their enthusiasm.

"I need your help in finding Pedro's murderers," I told Dona Pretiosa.

"El Grupo?"

I nodded. "Men working for El Grupo." I didn't want to tell her they were Russians. "If you can remember any of the other men who used to be part of Pedro's set, I'd like for you to give me their names." The singer had begun a new song, this one a slow ballad about lost love.

Dona Pretiosa shook her head slowly. "Before I would have refused to tell you," she said. "But now, after this, I don't know. How could his friends turn against Pedro?"

"They're a vicious group, Dona Pretiosa."

"They did not use to be. When I first knew them they were all kind, caring people. To think that those men who came here yesterday, hardened killers, work with those boys now! They wanted to overthrow the government *then*, and I thought they were right. That is why I let their group meet here. But why overthrow the government now? I do not understand. Pedro and other members of El Grupo used to meet here several years ago. There were about two dozen of them. Most I have not seen in years. A few continued coming here until a few months ago. Not for meetings, just as regular customers. They were good people."

"Not any more." I had to get her to break.

"I have been an idealist all my life, Mr. Bryan. Now, in the last few months I have lost this idealism. People speak of being disillusioned in their youth. I, who have always had hope in human nature and justice, am being disillusioned in my old age. I loved these men, as I love the other students and radicals who come to me." She glanced toward the crowd in the front of the room. "But I can no longer protect them. Not after I truly see what they're doing, their idea of revolution."

Suddenly a look of anger passed over Dona Pretiosa's face. She rose abruptly and went to the counter. She returned with a pen and a sheet of paper. She sat down and began writing. She wrote rapidly, angrily, as though attacking the paper itself. When she was finished, she handed the paper to me. I glanced at it. It contained seven names.

"These are all I can remember," she explained. "Two of the men on the list are among those who came here recently, but I remember them as being with Pedro in the old days. Others, I remember their names from back then. Most of the people who met with Pedro, I never knew their names, or I knew only their first names."

I thanked Dona Pretiosa and, rising, kissed her gently on the cheek. "What's lost is lost," the man sang in his high plaintive voice, "and will never come again."

As I came out of Dona Pretiosa's I was again accosted by a streetwalker. This one's skin-tight pants were red, and her hair was dark and thick.

"Why don't you come with me, goodlooker," she said, grabbing my arm.

"No thanks." I tried to brush her off, but the babe clung tenaciously. The grip of her lacquered fingers was strong.

"Come on, I'll give you what you want," she

said in a low, would-be sexy voice. She heaved her
jutting breasts against my chest.

"Look, lady," I said, "I told you I'm not interested. I don't want to make trouble, but I will if
you don't let go of me."

"I think you'd better go with the lady," a man's
voice said from behind me. I felt something hard
shoved into my back.

"You the pimp?" I asked without turning
around.

"Yeah, you can call me that," he answered
mockingly. "A pimp with a gun on you, fellow,
which is gonna blast right through you if you don't
do what the lady says. You believe me?" I believed
him.

"Whatever you say," I replied.

"Get in the car," the lady demanded. The seduc-
tiveness had disappeared from her voice. A cream-
colored sedan had pulled up beside us.

"I'd like to oblige you," I said. "But first tell me
where we're going. What's this all about? You
going to sell me into white slavery?"

"You've been wanting to meet with El Grupo
Febrero, Mr. Carter, well now you're going to
meet with them," the man said. He'd come from
behind and was on my left now. He was a large
heavily muscled young man with curly black hair
and a mustache. He was wearing the inevitable
blue jeans and a work shirt. He opened the car
door with one hand, still keeping the gun on me
with the other. A jab in my right rib told me that
my "streetwalker" had a gun too.

"Nice of you to grant me all my wishes," I said.
I looked around the street. It was crowded, but

there wasn't a cop in sight. No doubt abductions and worse were a pretty common occurence in the Barrio Chino, and yelling out to passerbys wasn't going to get me anything. Except maybe a bullet through my lungs.

"Search him before he gets in," the man said to the woman. She reached inside my coat and pulled out Wilhelmina. Then she patted me down. Her hands lingered at my crotch and she twisted my balls sadistically. But she missed Pierre, the cyanide gas bomb, which I keep taped to my left thigh. She also missed Hugo, the stilleto on my right forearm. And she missed the list of names from Dona Pretiosa, which I'd put under the band of my undershorts.

"Okay," the dark-haired woman said, and she and the man hustled me into the back seat of the car. They sat one on each side of me. We pulled away from the curb.

The third man in the car, the driver, was middle-aged and had a head as bald as an eagle, and a beak like an eagle too. He also wore a blue work shirt. I noted that the voice of the man beside me was coarse, with lower-class inflections, not at all like the voice of an educated man. He had deep acne pits on his face, and curly black hair grew up from his chest onto his neck. His hands, too, were covered with thick, dark hair. As for the woman, she'd dropped her hooker bit, but that didn't make her at all classy. On the contrary, I liked her a lot better as a common tart than as the gun-toting moll she'd suddenly become. Her face was moon-shaped and too fleshy. Her movements and manners were abrupt and crude, like those of a lady drill sergeant. And she chewed a big wad of gum, popping it against the inside of her mouth. Both the man and woman beside me were in their early thirties, but neither fit my idea of intellectual, former student revolutionaries, which is what we'd been led to believe the members of El Grupo were. But then, to coin a cliche, I guess you can't always judge a book by its cover. And I figured maybe the leaders of El Grupo had recruited members of the mythical "working class" for their dastardly schemes. In this case, the "proletariat" consisted of common thugs and criminals.

We were now well out of the Barrio Chino's crowded streets and heading away from the populated center of the city. It looked to me like we were going toward the amusement park at the top of Barcelona. Already the road we were on was becoming steeper and I could see the hilly region on the edge of town in the distance. I was surprised that the man and woman hadn't blindfolded me so that I wouldn't be able to see where they were taking me. But I figured this was a clue to their intentions. They didn't plan on me tracing this route after they let me go, because they didn't plan on letting me go: It was death they had in mind for me. Probably after slow torture. I thought of those photographs Lorca had showed me of El Grupo's previous victims: the split fingernails, the electrically scorched genitals and flesh, the broken limbs. I shuddered. I'd been trying to meet up with El Grupo ever since I got to Spain, and I was apparently finally being taken to them. The circumstances, to say the least, weren't exactly what I'd had in mind; but I'm adaptable.

The sedan was now climbing up the steep street
of a quiet, residential area. The houses to the left
and right were dark, indicating that the people who
lived here had long since gone to bed. Only an occasional street lamp broke the darkness. I glanced
to my left. The babe had gotten careless. She'd put
her own gun back in her purse and had been holding Wilhelmina on me since we got in the car. Only
now she'd laid Wilhelmina on her tightly trousered
lap as she unwrapped another stick of gum. She
wasn't even looking at me. I looked to my left. The
man's gun was still pointing at my chest. His black
eyes met mine.

"Won't be long now, Mr. Carter," he said, bar-
ing dirty, yellowed teeth. "Your mission in Spain
will be accomplished," he continued and poked the
barrel of his gun into my ribs for emphasis. I ignored his taunting. I had to keep calm and act
quickly. The driver had been picking up speed as
we climbed the hill, and the car must have been
hitting eighty by the time we got to the top. The
bald-headed man made no attempt to check the
sedan's speed as we started descending the hill.
There were no other cars on the long, narrow
street. Now was the time.

"Watch out, to your left," I yelled at the top of
my lungs. The driver gasped a startled "Wha. . ."
and braked violently. He didn't bring the sedan to
a complete halt, but the three of us in the back were
thrown forward. I heard Wilhelmina and the
woman's purse fall from her lap to the car floor.
The man to my left looked out the window at his
side. It was the opening I needed. I chopped on his
gun arm, and the gun dropped to the floor. Then I

brought my hand up and dealt him a sharp blow to the side of his neck that left him temporarily stunned. I turned to my other companion. She was bending down toward the floor, trying to retrieve the guns there. I rammed my fist into her lower back. She gasped and doubled over.

Fortunately the driver had pretty much lost control of the car when he'd braked, and all of his concentration now was devoted to keeping the sedan from crashing into the houses that lined the narrow street. The man in the back had recovered from my blow to his neck and grabbed my arm. I jerked free and slammed my fist into his face. As he yelled, blood ran out of his mouth, and I saw that I'd broken a couple of his yellow teeth. I reached over him for the door handle at his side. He saw what was coming for he immediately threw himself against me. But I managed to open the door. He wedged his feet between the floor and front seat of the car, trying to avoid being thrown out of the car.

"Stop it, you damn fool," the bald-headed guy in front yelled at me. "You're going to kill us all."

"That's what I had in mind," I yelled back as I pushed his buddy through the open door on his left. The man flew into the air ass-backwards, but one of his feet that he'd wedged against the front seat temporarily stopped his fall. Then I heard the ankle snap like a twig, and he cried out in pain. He'd grasped onto the swinging open door, but the pain from his broken ankle had sapped his power. As we hit a bump in the road, he lost his grip and his body was thrown, head first, into the side of a building.

I bent down to pick up Wilhelmina, which had

landed at my feet. It was then that I felt the woman
on my back. She grabbed my face and sunk her
sharp fingernails into my left cheek. With her other
hand she grabbed my right arm and pinioned it
against my back. With my free hand I reached behind me and grabbed at her thick head of hair. She
let out a howl of pain, but she pressed up harder on
my arm. For a moment there I thought she was
going to break it. Her five fingernails aimed at my
eye. I shut my eyes and grabbed one of her tits,
twisting it with every ounce of strength I had. She
howled again, and this time loosened her grasp.
The driver looked around to see what was happening. This caused him to lose control of the car
again, and the woman was thrown away from me.
She bent once again to retrieve her gun.

I looked up to see that we were approaching the
bottom of the hill. There was a stone wall there,
and the road veered sharply to the left. At the
speed we were going the driver would barely make
that turn—if he was lucky. I moved to the still open
door. I jumped just as the car turned the corner
and almost overturned. The abrupt angle caused
my body to be thrown back against the fender of
the car. An excruciating pain shot through my
right side, and for a second there I thought it was
all over, that I was going to fall beneath the car's
back wheels. But then I felt the car move away
from me, and I hit the cobblestone street with a
heavy thud. A knifelike pain went through my
body from the top of my head to my feet. I heard
bullets ricocheting around me, their impact against
the stone street echoing in the night's silence. The
woman was firing on me from the sedan. But her

aim was bad. Looking up, I saw why. The car was still lurching down the street from side to side. It seemed to still be out of control. Soon it disappeared in the distance. I guess she and the bald man had decided they didn't want to come after me again. At least not tonight.

I must have passed out for a few seconds. The next thing I saw were lights going on in the nearby houses, and I heard excited voices. For a while I just lay there on the cold stones. I heard doors being opened and the excited voices coming closer to me. My bones were probably broken, I thought, but I forced myself to try to sit up. I managed to lift myself to a sitting position. I was amazed. My body felt like hell, but at least that meant no broken bones. A man wearing a pair of trousers over his nightshirt and carrying a lantern approached me.

"Where's a telephone?" I heard myself asking, in a low, weak voice.

In the distance I heard a woman screaming. "A dead man," she cried, "a dead man." She kept repeating this hysterical litany. Apparently the man in the workshirt had been less lucky in his fall from the car than I.

Chapter Nine

I was awakened by a knock on the door of my pension. I looked at the clock: 10:30 a.m. The painkiller I'd taken the night before had knocked me out immediately, and kept me knocked out longer than I'd planned. My shoulder felt like hell, a burning mass of flesh and muscles. As I got out of bed, a sharp pain shot through my right leg. I walked, naked, to the door.

"Who is it?" I asked groggily.

"Pilar," came my friend's low, sexy voice. I opened the door and let her in, not bothering to cover myself. Hell, she'd seen my body before. Pilar's eyes widened as she came into the room.

"My God, Nick, you look awful." Her eyes moved from my face down my naked body. "I mean," she laughingly corrected herself, "your face is in pretty bad shape. Your body, as usual, looks terrific."

"Thanks," I said, "but the body doesn't feel very terrific." I glanced in the mirror over the sink. Pilar was certainly right about my face. There was a large bruise, blue and swollen, along the left side of my face where I'd hit the cobblestones when I

jumped out of the car. And there were long red
scratches along my left cheek and my neck where
the "hooker" had got her claws into me.

"Poor darling," Pilar said, gently touching my
swollen face. "El Grupo was pretty brutal to you
last night, weren't they?"

"How'd you guess?"

"Just women's intuition," she said. "And besides, I talked to Lorca this morning. He told me
you'd called late last night." I asked Pilar if Lorca
had given her any more news on the case. The only
new information was that last night El Grupo had
indeed claimed responsibility for the bombing of
the post office in Talavera de la Reina yesterday.
And they'd completely avoided Lorca's sentries at
all the media centers. This time they'd left their
taped communique on the altar of a church in a
small town south of Madrid. A priest had found it
when he'd come in this morning to do matins. It
was as though the villains had anticipated Lorca's
orders. Or else they had an informant somewhere
within the government or the police.

Also, Lorca had already checked out the list of
names from Dona Pretiosa that I'd relayed to him
last night. His men had been at work all night, and
they'd come up with the last known addresses of all
seven of these members of El Grupo, and also the
addresses of the known relatives of five of them.
The best thing for Pilar and I to do today would be
to find the men or at least quiz the relatives.

But just for a moment I didn't want to have to
think about El Grupo. Not while I was standing
naked in front of a woman who was looking more
beautiful than ever this morning. Even in a dump

like this pension Pilar retained that air of elegance and slight mystery that I found so appealing. I looked into those deep green eyes, and I guess she knew what I wanted. For her hand moved from my cheek to my shoulder, and then she began caressing my back. Despite everything, despite the pain and the grogginess in my head from the painkiller, Pilar's touch aroused me tremendously.

I bent to kiss her, and her tongue played gently against my lips. She ran her fingers across my chest and succeeded in exciting me even further.

"I think I'd better go back to bed," I said teasingly.

"I agree," Pilar said in her husky, sexy growl. "You have to take care of yourself, build up your strength." As I moved toward the bed, I felt a stab of pain go through my body once again. But a woman like Pilar can make you forget even the most horrific aches. At least for a while. I lay back on the bed.

"Join me," I said to Pilar, who was now standing, facing me at the end of the bed. Slowly she undid the buttons of her light crepe blouse, looking into my face all the while. It was as though she was doing a strip tease in slow motion, with all the vulgarity removed. She opened the front of her blouse. God, were those breasts beautiful!

Still very slowly and sensuously, she reached behind and undid the zipper of her linen skirt. The skirt fell to the floor, revealing a pair of silk stockings held up by a small garter belt, and white lace panties that accentuated her bronzed curves. Her hands lingered around her navel as she played with the elastic at the top of the panties, then she inched them down her legs and stepped out of them.

Still at the foot of the bed, she turned, like a re-volving statue, so that I'd have the chance to take in her whole body: the breasts, the slim waist, the delicate curves where the shoulder-blades met the back, the rounded softness of the buttocks. She moved to the side of the bed and stood looking down at me. Then she bent toward me, so that I could take first one and then the other of her breasts into my mouth as I lay on my back. I moved my hand between her thighs, and Pilar moaned softly. When I had finished kissing and licking her breasts, Pilar stood up straight again and I let my tongue play along her torso and belly. Then she kicked off her shoes and climbed onto the bed.

I turned to meet Pilar's body and again I felt a jab of pain in my right side. Involuntarily I groaned.

"No, Nick," Pilar said. "Don't exert yourself. This time I work to please you. Lay back." I did as she wanted me to, and Pilar moved onto my body, straddling me. I groaned with pleasure now as she slowly eased my body into hers. She bent her head toward mine, and her long golden hair fell across my chest. Our lips met and our tongues probed deeply into each other's mouths as she moved up and down on my groin.

Then Pilar drew her mouth away from mine and straightened her back. She rode me, like a little girl on a stallion. I looked up and watched her face be-come wilder and more ecstatic as the speed of our rhythmn increased. I thrust my body upward, higher and higher, into her. She threw back her

head, tossing her hair in the air and groaning softly. The higher I thrust the more pleasure I got, and
the more loudly Pilar cried out. Finally, in one
electrifying moment, we both climaxed, and Pilar
collapsed into my arms.

We lay in bed, still naked, and glanced over the
list of men we'd gotten from Dona Pretiosa and
their addresses we'd gotten from Lorca. We split
up the names, I taking four, Pilar taking three.
We'd work separately, first visiting the last known
addresses of the men. It seemed unlikely that we'd
find any of El Grupo at these addresses, but we
hoped we might get some information from a
neighbor or landlord. Then we'd visit, again separately, the relatives on Lorca's other list. Perhaps
we could persuade the men's families to tell us
what—if anything—they knew about El Grupo.

As we plotted our strategy, Pilar took out one of
the small, thin cigarettes she smoked. I reached for
a lighter from the bedside table, but Pilar had already taken a match out of her purse. As she struck
the match and brought the flame to the end of her
cigarette, I followed her hand, mesmerized. My
heart felt like it was going to stop for a second and
my stomach felt like it had turned upside down as
I watched the cigarette catch fire and Pilar exhale
the pale, bluish smoke. The still flaming match she
was holding between her fingers was long and narrow and silver. I'd seen a match like that exactly
once before in my life: when I'd gotten it out of the
pocket of the El Grupo brute who Maria killed.
Pilar flicked her wrist to put out the flame and
tossed the match into the bedside ashtray.
Goosebumps rose on my arms.

"Anything wrong?" Pilar asked casually. She put her hand to my face and began to caress me again, only now her touch seemed leaden, cold, repulsive.

"No," I lied, stalling for time. Was anything *wrong*? Plenty. A whirl of images suddenly rushed through my head, like pictures in a newsreel gone out of control. I replayed the events of the last few days, and suddenly everything was cast in a new, sinister light. Some of the mystery of El Grupo's affairs could be explained by that match lying in the ashtray beside my bed, and if true, the explanation wasn't pretty.

Where had someone first tried to kill me after I'd arrived in Spain? At Pilar's party. Neither the police or Lorca's men could come up with any leads that suggested either the guests or the servants knew my identity and would want to do me in. However, no one, including myself, had thought to investigate the other person at that party, who *did* know my real identity: my hostess.

At the beach yesterday, Pilar had shot down two men from El Grupo, rather than capturing them. Maybe she had to kill them, maybe she didn't. In any case, her bullets had prevented us from quizzing them about their organization.

When we'd returned from the beach our rooms had been ransacked. Except no one was supposed to know where we were staying. How had they found out? Could the lady herself have alerted someone?

Last night I'd been puzzled when the man and woman had suddenly appeared at Dona Pretiosa's to abduct me, especially since the only person I'd told I was going there was Pilar. If they'd been alerted to grab me there, only one person could have alerted them.

Throughout the case it had seemed highly probable that either the government or someone in Lorca's network had been leaking information to El Grupo, the latest example being their avoidance of all the media centers at precisely the time Lorca had placed guards there. What better person to pass on privileged information than one of Lorca's agents herself?

The answers to all of my questions pointed in one direction. The direction led to the woman in bed beside me. La Condesa, Double-Agent.

I remembered Pilar's past. She had freely confessed, the first night I'd met her, that she had been something of a student revolutionary. It now made perfect sense that she could well have been a member of a student activist group like . . . El Grupo. Of course, Pilar had obviously proved herself a top agent, working for Lorca. But I've been in this profession long enough to know that that had a certain logic too. If agents of one organization set out to infiltrate another organization, they try to be the best in the organization they're secretly working against. Because the higher up in the structure they go, the more damage they can do, the more important is the information that they pass on. Also, Pilar's seeming attachment to me, emotional and physical, would all be part of the game too. From Cleopatra down to Mata Hari there's been a long tradition of female spies sleeping with and even pretending to love men they can get information from. Looking at this beautiful woman beside me,

I felt like I'd been enveloped in a small, personal nightmare, inside the larger nightmare of El Grupo. Except if my conjectures were right, the two nightmares were one; they converged in the person of Pilar. I was furious at her and at myself for being taken in. I grabbed La Condesa by the wrist.

"Wasn't once enough for you?" she laughed. As I increased the pressure on her wrist, her laugher faded. She discovered it wasn't sex I was after this time.

"Where did you get that match?" I said. She glanced at the long silver article in the ashtray.

"At Juan's. Why?"

"The truth," I said, increasing the pressure on her wrist. Tears were beginning to appear in her green eyes.

"I got that match at Juan's, Nick. You're hurting me. What's wrong with you?"

I let go of her wrist. I had to play this one cool. What if she was telling the truth and had gotten the match at Ruiz's mansion? Perhaps the two of them were working together. I remembered their conspiratorial glances that night at Pilar's party. Also, I remembered what a strange "coincidence" it was that Ruiz had happened to arrive in Barcelona just as we did. And that phony search through our hotel rooms had made it very convenient indeed for Pilar to stay with him.

I looked straight into Pilar's bright green eyes. "And are you sleeping with Ruiz too?" I asked levelly. Pilar's slap across my face was quick and strong. The blow stung my already bruised cheek. Pilar jumped out of bed, throwing the sheets back against me. Her slow-motion striptease of an hour before was reversed. She began dressing; her gestures were quick and jerky.

"Tell me about your relationship with El Conde," I said as she pulled on her stockings.

"I'd heard about your reputation as a ladykiller, Mr. Carter," she said, "but I hadn't been warned that you were also a jealous fool. My relationship with El Conde Ruiz is none of your business."

"It's very much my business," I said, and I repeated, this time more forcefully. "Tell me about your relationship, all of it. I want the truth."

Pilar must have sensed through my tone of voice, that this time I really meant business.

"All right," she said, her voice seething with anger and sarcasm, "you want to know about Juan, I'll tell you."

"Go ahead."

Pilar continued dressing as she talked. "Juan Ruiz was a close friend of Carlos, my late husband. They were, in fact, childhood friends. They grew up in the same milieu and later they attended the same military boarding school. They remained very close until they were in college, then they went their separate ways and had many disagreements, mainly over politics. Carlos, as you know, was a democrat, while Juan leaned toward the right. Later, after college, Juan became a member of the Franco government and he eventually worked upward into a high position in the Department of Defense. Ironically, when we finally achieved democracy and my husband became a Minister, Juan was dismissed from his post because his right-wing ideas were unsympathetic to the new Prime Minister. But I suppose you're not interested in the politics, are you Mr. Carter? It's the dirt you want."

Pilar was now standing before the dirty mirror

above my sink, combing those long blond tresses. She turned her head toward me, waiting for an answer. But when I ignored her sarcasm and remained silent, she turned her eyes back to her own reflection and continued.

"Well, you'll be disappointed to know that there is no dirt. Despite their political disagreements, Juan and my husband continued seeing one another over the years. They had their childhood ties, and the Spanish aristocracy is really a very small world. After I married Carlos, I naturally occasionally saw Juan too—because of my position as Carlos's wife, of course, but also because Juan and I had much in common—music, art—and I found him sympathetic.

"Then, after Carlos died Juan was very kind and very attentive. It took me a while to realize that Juan's interest in me was becoming more than just friendly. One day, to my enormous surprise, Juan actually proposed to me. He said he'd been in love with me for years. I don't know whether he meant he'd been in love with me while Carlos was alive or only afterwards. I didn't want to know. Of course, a marriage between Juan and me was out of the question. I'd certainly never been attracted to him, and I told him so. I also told him that if he persisted I wouldn't see him at all any more.

"Juan, unlike some people I can mention, has always been a perfect gentleman. He agreed to never bring up the subject of marriage again. For about six months he didn't call; perhaps he was more hurt than I'd realized. Then one day I ran into him at a concert and we talked. Everything between us was just like it had been before my husband died, and we became friendly again—not intimate, but friendly. I now go to his parties, he comes to mine, and we see each other at concerts and shows and that sort of thing. And that's the extent of our 'relationship.' "

Pilar came to the bed, picked up the list of names she was to visit that afternoon, and looking down at me asked, "Anymore questions?"

It was a very pretty story she'd told, complete with hero and heroine, and it may even have been a true story, but it didn't explain the silver match and Pilar's activities of the last few days.

"Yes, a few more questions," I answered her.

"They can wait, I'm sure," Pilar said icily as she headed toward the door.

I leaped out of bed and blocked the doorway. "I'd like to know more about your activities as a student," I said. "For example, is it possible that you knew any members of El Grupo while you were in college? That perhaps you were a member of El Grupo yourself?" There it was, I had to ask it, but it was one of the toughest questions I'd ever had to ask. Pilar's eyes widened and she stared into my face for what seemed an eternity. She raised one arm, and I thought she was going to slap me again. But then she let her arm drop, and turning her back on me, she walked back into the center of the room. I followed her and picked up the silver match from the ashtray. "And I'd like some more information about this," I said, holding out the match. Pilar turned to face me. Her eyes were glistening with tears, her expression was pained and puzzled.

"How can you . . ." Her voice faltered, and then she recovered. She angrily brushed the tears from her eyes. "Of course I don't know any members of

El Grupo, and no, I was never a member of El Grupo. But it's obvious that you no longer trust me. Why I don't know, but you'd better call Lorca. Ask him to assign another Spanish agent to work with you. I quit. As for that damned match, like I said, I picked it up at Juan's." Pilar's tears and then her anger were genuine. I was beginning to believe that she had been telling me the truth.

"I'm sorry," I said, taking her hand, "but I had to put you through this, just to make certain you really are on my side."

"But why, Nick?"

"This," I said, looking down at the match. "It's exactly like the match I found in the pocket of the man who tried to kill Maria."

"Oh God!" The surprise on Pilar's face was real. "But what does it mean?"

"I don't know," I said, taking Pilar in my arms. I'd been hard on her, for the sake of the case. I'd had to be absolutely certain I was getting the truth from her. But now I just wanted to comfort her. I explained my doubts to her and the reasons for them. After Pilar had heard the explanation for my questions, she didn't resent the harshness I'd used. She was a real pro all right. She clarified the events of yesterday. Her more detailed account of her chase of the men at the cabana and at the beach made clear that she'd really had no alternative but to shoot them.

The question about why one of the men from El Grupo had one of El Conde Ruiz's matches was as much a puzzlement to Pilar as it was to me. How had he got it?

Suddenly two facts occurred to me. One, *Ruiz* had been at Pilar's party when someone tried to kill me; it could very well have been him. Two, last night I'd called Pilar at Ruiz's mansion; it was then that I'd told her I was going to Dona Pretiosa's. If someone, Ruiz for example, had been listening in on our conversation over an extension, that would explain how the men who'd kidnapped me knew where I'd be.

The match, the shooting at Pilar's, the kidnapping last night—all seemed to link El Conde Ruiz to El Grupo. But the connection was only circumstantial and it seemed almost beyond belief. Ruiz was, and according to Pilar always had been, a member of the far right; El Grupo, on the other hand, was as far to the left as you could go. The old bromide about politics making strange bedfellows is often true enough, but I'd never encountered any political bedfellows who were *this* strange. It was almost inconceivable that a man of Ruiz's background and professed politics could be a secret member of a revolutionary terrorist organization. Yet how else could we explain the evidence that we had?

It occurred to me that if Ruiz was somehow connected with El Grupo, it wasn't the safest thing in the world to have Pilar staying in his house. Ruiz had known Pilar was in Barcelona. If he also knew that she was an agent, it could possibly have been him who'd ransacked our rooms: to lure Pilar into his house. I wanted Pilar out of that house. Pilar, however, disagreed.

"Look," she argued, "if Juan is, in fact, connected with El Grupo, the best thing for me to do now is to pretend that I suspect nothing. If I leave his place abruptly, he'll know that something's up. Besides, there's a good possibility—if Juan is involved—that I can find out why, can pick up some clues, by checking out the house and observing him."

I had to hand it to Pilar for courage, and she was right about staying in the house, despite the danger involved.

"I just wish I could observe El Conde Ruiz too," I said ruefully, "and be around to help you."

"But you can Nick!" Pilar explained that tonight Ruiz had invited a number of people to his estate for a buffet dinner followed by a chamber music concert. Pilar would tell him that she'd run into me in a gallery today and ask if she might invite me to the party. She'd explain what a music buff I was, and besides I'd want to get a chance to see his mansion, one of the famous showplaces of Europe. I'd be invited, of course, as David Bryan, New York architect. Even if Ruiz knew my real identity, he could hardly refuse Pilar's request for an invitation for me without raising unwelcome questions about his motives. Pilar would call him this afternoon. In the meantime, we agreed to set off on our investigative journeys and to meet later in the afternoon to compare notes on Dona Pretiosa's men.

That afternoon, as I visited the houses and apartments of the men Dona Pretiosa had given me, and talked to the men's landlords, neighbors, and relatives, some curious new facts came to light. Patterns began to emerge about El Grupo, but they were baffling patterns.

First, of the four men on my list, not one of them was to be found. Two of the men had lived alone in apartments. From their neighbors and the buildings' managers, I learned that both men had disappeared suddenly without giving notice, without saying so much as a word. Neither man had bothered to have his phone or electricity shut off, and each had left all of his possessions behind. The evidence indicated that both men had left abruptly and unexpectedly.

"Place was a mess," said one of the apartment managers, "why Juan even left behind dirty dishes in the sink, and at least a week's worth of garbage in the bin. Not like him to go off half-cocked like that." Except for cleaning up, the manager had left Juan's apartment untouched, hoping that Juan, a favorite tenant of his, would return. When I told him I was from the police, the man allowed me to inspect the apartment. Juan was a lawyer, and I found nothing unusual in his modern, rather messy bachelor flat. Law books and legal briefs were everywhere, but there was nothing—not even a socialist magazine—to indicate that he was a member of any kind of revolutionary group. The only items I found in the apartment that might be of use to us were a couple of snapshots that the manager identified as being of Juan. I pocketed them.

The manager of the second man's apartment building, an older and obviously less expensive place, said that when his tenant Carlos, hadn't returned after a month, he'd auctioned off the man's belongings. He didn't have an address of any of Carlos's relatives and felt that the sale of Carlos's belongings would make up for the month's rent that he'd lost. Yet aside from the lurch the manager obviously felt Carlos had left him in, he had only good things to say about his former tenant, who was a school teacher.

I, more fortunate than his landlord, did have the address of Carlos's mother. But about all I got out of her was a photograph of her son, and I think she gave that to me so that I'd stop asking questions about him. She was transparently nervous throughout our talk, and she claimed that Carlos was in the south, taking a vacation because of "his health." When I pressed her for further details about just where in the south Carlos was and exactly what was wrong with his health, she became first vague and then indignant. It was pretty obvious the whole story was a lie. Whether she was lying out of fear or because she'd been told to, I couldn't tell. All I knew was that she was damned worried about her son, and not just because of my questions.

The third man on my list, Esteban, had lived with his family. His mother and father told me that Esteban was "traveling in America," but they couldn't be specific about his itineary, said they didn't know. They spoke in the same fearful, tentative tones of Carlos's mother, and they claimed they didn't even have a photograph of their son! They were scared all right. They did volunteer the information that Esteban was also a schoolteacher, and even gave me the name of the school where he'd taught.

When I checked with the school, I found out that Esteban had disappeared on exactly the same day as Juan and Carlos. That day Esteban simply hadn't showed up for his classes. He'd given no notice, no warning. When the principal had called on Esteban's parents they'd told him that Esteban had gone to Sevilla to care for his sick grandfather and would be away indefinitely. They'd given the school a different story from the one they'd given me: both stories were clearly false. The school supplied me with a photograph of Esteban, taken from their employee files.

My final visit that afternoon was to the wife of

the fourth man on my list, Miguel. The couple's
two small children, a smiling little boy of three, and
a pale beautiful girl-child of four, played with a top
at our feet as their mother and I discussed their
father. We sat in the living room of their small,
sunny house. The woman, Juanita, was young and
pretty, but she seemed tired and harried, like someone unused to raising two small children on her
own. She readily admitted her husband's puzzling
disappearance, and she spoke bitterly of his leaving
her alone with the children. The three of them had
been surviving for the last couple of months on
food and clothing provided by Juanita's in-laws.
When I asked, she forthrightly admitted that her
husband had been a member of El Grupo when he
was a student at the University of Barcelona.

Juanita recounted her husband's disappearance,
with hardly any prompting from me. One night
Miguel hadn't come home from the pharma-
ceutical house where he worked as a chemist. At
first, Juanita simply thought he had been delayed,
but as the hours passed, and she got no answer
when she phoned his company, she began to worry.
By midnight she was frantic and had decided to
phone the police. Then she received a telephone
call. A man, whose voice she didn't recognize, told
Juanita that her husband was now working for a
revolutionary organization, El Grupo Febrero,
and that he would be away for awhile. The man
told her that if she didn't want her husband to die,
she wouldn't call the police or mention this call to
anyone. Juanita immediately went to her in-laws
and told them what had happened. She still wanted
to call the police, but Miguel's parents persuaded
her to wait. The next morning, Juanita heard, over
the radio, about El Grupo's first bloody kidnap-

ping. Again, she thought she should go to the police, and over the next weeks as the chronicle of El Grupo's terrorist activities took over the headlines, she became more and more convinced that she had to go to the police with her story. For one thing, she didn't really believe that her husband was taking part in such unimaginable horrors. And I got the impression, although Juanita didn't come right out and say this, that if her husband *was* part of such murderous activities, then he *deserved* to be turned in. Each time, however, Juanita spoke of going to the police, his parents dissuaded her. They threatened to cut off all support to Juanita and her children if she talked to anyone about their son's disappearance.

"So you see, I really had no choice," Juanita said. "My children had to eat." Yet, I got the impression that Juanita was immensely relieved to be unburdening herself to me after having this gut-wrenching secret bottled up for so long. She gave me a photograph of Miguel and begged me to please find her husband; her children needed their father back. I promised Juanita I'd do the best I could. I didn't tell her that if Miguel ever came back to her, it would probably be in a coffin.

I met Pilar at 3:30 in the vestibule of the church of La Sacra Familia. La Sacra Familia is an enormous gothic structure, designed by the great Barcelonian architect Gaudi over fifty years ago. As Pilar and I walked through the cathedral's winding corridors with their bizarrely curved walls and their outlandish stone carvings, I felt as though we were in a physical paradigm of this case: twisted walls stretching out in all directions, with unfathomable icons everywhere, and with no exit in sight.

Pilar's investigations had revealed the same patterns as mine. All the men she'd checked on had disappeared abruptly shortly before the first attacks of El Grupo; all the men had been students several years ago at the university here; all had recently been (seemingly) successful young professionals; the families of all the men had been silent or had made up unconvincing stories to cover their sons' going underground. After talking to Juanita, I was pretty certain that the men's families had all gotten the same threatening phone call that she had. If you mention your husband's (or son's, or brother's) disappearance, he'll die. That explained the fear I'd seen on the relatives's faces and the conspiracy of silence. What it didn't explain was how these men could emotionally blackmail their own families. In a way the psychological terrorism the members of El Grupo were practicing on their families was even more appalling than their public terrorism. They were an unspeakably evil lot.

Pilar added the set of photographs she'd gathered to my own, and we both agreed that none of the men in these seven pictures resembled any of the members of El Grupo we'd so far encountered. Perhaps these were the masterminds behind the operation and didn't venture out in public. In any case, I'd take all of the photographs to Barcelona Intelligence Headquarters so that they could be copied and relayed on to Lorca.

While I did that Pilar would return to El Conde Ruiz's. She'd called him this afternoon, and he had said he'd be "delighted" to see me this evening. Yeah, I'd be delighted too, especially if we could find some further clue to link him to El Grupo.

At Barcelona Intelligence Headquarters, I gave the men in the lab the photographs, and placed a call to Lorca while I waited for them to be copied. I described the latest developments, and Lorca once again vouched for Pilar's absolute reliability and trustworthiness. He didn't know much about El Conde Ruiz, but he said he'd soon find out all there was to know. He would open a file on him immediately, and send his men around to interview Ruiz's former government associates this afternoon. The only political link Lorca could see between El Grupo was that they both hated the government: El Grupo because they were anarchistic hooligans; Ruiz because he disagreed with the policies of and had been dismissed from the present government.

Lorca liked the idea of Pilar and I being at Ruiz's together tonight, although he emphasized that it could be an extremely dangerous situation— if Ruiz knew that we were both agents.

"Well, most situations in this job are extremely dangerous," I said.

"That they are," Lorca laughed. "But I'd hate to lose my top agent. And Hawk would never forgive me if I lost you. Seriously, Nick, give me a call after you leave the party. If I don't hear from either you or Pilar by morning, I'll send a search team to Ruiz's estate. And remember, this is Thursday, El Grupo promised to strike as 'high as they can go' by Saturday. If this doesn't break tonight or tomorrow, it may be too late."

Chapter Ten

"Did you see the Picasso?" the tall, shapely brunette asked me.

"It's from his Blue Period," said her companion, a tall, thin man wearing glasses.

I was standing with them and with Pilar in the drawing room of El Conde Ruiz's mansion. I had arrived about twenty minutes before and had been greeted graciously by a smiling El Conde Ruiz and by Pilar. She was serving as his hostess for the evening, and she looked stunningly beautiful in a long white tube of a dress that set off her fine shoulders and breasts. El Conde Ruiz had told me he was glad I could make it, and he hoped he could get my opinion of his house, which he described as a blend of the traditional and the contemporary. The place was certainly the "showplace" Pilar had described. Situated on a many-acred estate, the main house must have been at least five or six hundred years old. The Moorish influence was predominant, with red tiles and stucco and elaborately curled gargoyles gracing the mansion's front exterior. Inside, however, Ruiz had completely transformed the building's centuries-old ambiance. The decor was glaringly modern with marble floors and chrome and glass furniture and bright modern paintings against the austere white walls. The entire back of the original structure had been knocked out and replaced by a wall of glass.

Pilar had suggested that she take me on a tour of the entire house. El Conde had smilingly agreed, and had then excused himself to check with the musicians who were now setting up their instruments in the music room for his concert. El Conde Ruiz was certainly a connoisseur—of music and art and beautiful women. And of revolutionary groups?

Pilar had shown me through a spectacular black leather and chrome library and most of the rooms on the ground floor. We had been constantly greeted by the other guests, all of whom seemed to know Pilar well.

"They're mainly art and music people," she had whispered to me, "with just the right number of 'society' people thrown in for good measure." The problem was that Pilar was so popular she and I hadn't had a chance to talk alone since I'd arrived. The tall couple we were with now, who apparently fell into the "art" category, were nattering happily along about El Conde Ruiz's art collection, "the best modern one in Spain." They seemed reluctant to let me go until they had recounted the history and price tag of every painting in the room.

"If you'll excuse us," Pilar said to them, "I want Mr. Bryan to have a chance to see the upstairs rooms before the concert begins." And she took me firmly by the arm and led me out of the drawing room. She stared straight ahead, avoiding looking at the people we passed so we wouldn't have to stop and chit-chat with them.

In the main entrance hall we approached a grand staircase, which was itself a minor work of art—chrome and marble. At the bottom of the staircase stood a liveried butler, an enormous man with a bulging forehead and extremely deep-set eyes. He asked if he could help us, and Pilar explained that I was an architect and that she was giving me a tour of the house. The man didn't look too pleased; perhaps he wanted the pleasure of showing off the house himself. At the top of the stairs Pilar led me down a glistening marble corridor full of modernistic sculptures. We went into an upstairs sitting room, closing the door behind us.

"What gives?" I asked immediately.

"Nice expressions you Americans have," Pilar laughed. "Actually I can't find anything concrete here. When I returned home this afternoon, Juan was, fortunately, out. So I had a chance to search all the rooms. The servants were around, of course, but I'm a good sneak and I managed to avoid them. At least I don't think anyone saw me scurrying in and out of rooms. Anyway, I knew the downstairs rooms pretty well already and, as I expected, I didn't find anything unusual there. Ditto the upstairs guest rooms. My hopes were pinned on Ruiz's private suite—his bedroom and office."

"Anything there?"

"Not much. I did manage to open the safe in his office, but all I found there were some routine real estate documents and bonds. I also checked his locked desk and again everything was routine. I photographed the pages of his address book," she said, handing me a roll of film, "but I don't think that will be very helpful. I recognized most of the names, including my own. But you might as well have Lorca develop it and see if anything new checks out."

"A complete washout," I said glumly.

"No, not entirely. As you probably would imagine, the grounds here are extensive, and I went exploring there too. Come here." Pilar took my hand and we moved to the glass wall of the room. It looked down onto a gorgeous vista of sloping lawns at the bottom of which was a brightly-lighted swimming pool. In the distance you could see the ocean and a full moon.

"Now look, Nick, to the left of the pool is the pool house." It was a large glass and chrome building. "It's a very elaborate place," Pilar continued. "Juan often entertains there and it has extra guest quarters. This afternoon I checked it out, when I was ostensibly showering and changing out of my swimsuit. Nothing there. Now, look to the right of the pool, in that clump of trees. There's another building." I looked and could barely make out a smaller, stone structure, which somewhat resembled the Moorish front of the main house.

"What is it?" I asked.

"An old carriage-house, supposedly. This afternoon, after I'd checked out the pool house, I wandered over there. It's an old building. I tried the door, which was locked. Then something strange happened. One of the gardeners, or anyway someone who said he was a gardener, came rushing over to me. I don't know where he suddenly appeared from, but he was very alarmed. He told me the building wasn't used anymore and not to bother trying to get in. What was so peculiar was the alarm in his face and voice, alarm amounting almost to terror. I mean, why did he come running up to me in such a hurry to prevent me from getting in? Especially since the building was locked anyway? What was he afraid I'd find? Why was he so upset?

"Then, I went back up to the house, I looked back down that way—my bedroom also faces in this direction. There Juan was coming up the slope, although I'd been told he wasn't home. I went downstairs to the terrace and greeted him when he reached the house. Casually I asked him where he was coming from. Juan said he'd been swimming, except I knew he hadn't been at the pool, because I'd been there. So I suspect that if there's anything here that's going to help us, it's in that carriage house. Where else could Juan have been?"

"When can we check out the carriage house?" I asked.

"I could do it tonight, after Juan goes to bed."

"No, that may be too late. We'd better do it while I'm here."

"Okay," Pilar said, "but you'll have to do it alone. I'm supposed to be Juan's hostess, and I have to sit with him at the concert and again at dinner. If you're not at dinner, you'll be missed too. So the only thing that could work is if you slip out during the concert and go down there then."

"I'll try," I said, "how long is the concert supposed to last?"

"It's scheduled to be about an hour."

"Doesn't give me much time." At this moment

we were interrupted by a knock on the door. Pilar glanced at me and whispered, "You can get to the lawn by the door in the library." Then she raised her voice and said, "Come in."

El Conde Ruiz opened the door and entered the room. "Ah, there you are," he said, "The butler told me you two had come up here. I just wanted to let you know that the musicians are going to begin in about five mintues."

"We'd better come down then," said Pilar, "I was just showing Mr. Bryan the Mondrian." She indicated a small black and white geometric abstract painting hanging above a sofa near us.

"Very fine," I said.

"Thank you," said Ruiz. I then asked him about the engineering involved in fitting the back glass wall into the existing structure of his house. Apparently I'd touched a point of Ruiz's vanity for he responded enthusiastically and went into a discourse about the difficulty and the ultimate satisfaction of having the glass wall installed.

As we turned to leave the room, Ruiz said to me, "By the way, Mr. Bryan," (did I detect a faint, ironic inflection of my name?) "how did you happen to come to Spain in the midst of our present troubles?"

"You mean El Grupo?" I looked into his eyes. They were cold.

"Yes, El Grupo. I've heard that tourism since they began their campaign has fallen by almost one hundred percent, but here you are. You must be a very brave man."

"Well," I said, "perhaps not so brave. I'd planned my trip here for several months, and I *do* have work to do. I didn't want to delay because of a group of hooligans. Besides, I have faith that your country will very soon be out of these people's clutches."

"Indeed?" Ruiz said. This time the note of irony in his voice was faint but unmistakable. "You're very optimistic, Mr. Bryan."

"That's the thing about us Americans," I replied. "Haven't you heard about how optimistic we are?"

Ruiz laughed. "That I have heard," he said, "although—and you must not take this personally Mr. Bryan—sometimes I feel that you Americans overstep yourselves. That you are, perhaps, too optimistic for your own good." There was now the slightest hint of a threat in Ruiz's tone. "Perhaps," he continued, "you should not be so certain that things will work out as you would like them to work out."

"Perhaps," I said, "but for the good of your country I hope I'm right."

"Yes. For the good of the country," Ruiz said dryly. Then he walked out of the room. "Shall we go listen to some Vivaldi, then," he said in the corridor, his smile returning.

As the three of us reached the bottom of the marble and chrome staircase, Ruiz announced to his guests that the music was ready to begin, and, with Pilar on his arm, he led them into yet another stunning room. This one had mirrored walls and ceiling and a pink marble floor. The five man chamber ensemble was sitting at the back of the room, near the glass wall, and chrome and leather chairs were arranged in front of them for the guests. I lingered at the entrance until most of the people were seated, then took a place at the back of the room, near the door.

Ruiz gave an elegant little speech, introducing the muscians, and then the sharp, almost cold strains of the seventeenth century music began. As I listened, I plotted my evening's itinerary. I recognized the Vivaldi piece, a piano and violin concerto, and I knew that it lasted about twelve minutes. At the end of this first piece, I would slip out of the room, hopefully unnoticed, and head down to the carriage house. That would give me about forty mintues to check things out there and make it back to the music room before the concert ended and dinner began. If I found anything of interest in the carriage house, I could return this evening after the guests had left and Ruiz and household had gone to sleep.

As the Vivaldi concerto ended, the guests broke into enthusiastic applause. I rose and headed for the door. I made it into the hallway unobserved, but there I ran into the bulging-forehead butler who had greeted Pilar and me earlier.

"May I help you sir?" he asked, eyeing me with icy disdain.

"The men's room," I said.

"It's on the second floor, sir, follow me." The library was only a few doors down from the music room, and that's where I needed to go. But if I didn't want to raise suspicions and perhaps abort my sortey into the night completely, I now had to follow the butler. He led me to the stairs.

"At the top of the stairs and to your right, Sir," he said. I began the ascent. Halfway up the stairs,

I turned and looked back. The butler was still standing at the bottom of the stairs staring up at me. I smiled at him and continued up the stairs. At the top of the stairs I turned left and then moving quickly to the far wall of the corridor (where the butler couldn't see me from below) I doubled back and ducked into the sitting room where Pilar and I had been earlier. I let myself out of the room's sliding glass doors onto a narrow terrace. I looked down. It was about a hundred foot jump to the lawn below, but I figured it was my only chance to get out of the house. I'd lost too much time already to try to sneak back down to the library, and besides, I figured the butler was probably still waiting for me at the bottom of the stairs.

The only real problem I could anticipate concerned the location of my landing. From what I could calculate of the house's layout, this room was one flight above, and horizontally somewhere between the music room and the library. That meant it was directly above either the dining room or the drawing room. Chances were that the servants were now preparing supper in the dining room and they might also be picking up drinks and ashtrays in the drawing room. In other words, someone might see me as I jumped past the glass windows of the rooms below. It was a chance I had to take. I climbed over a chrome railing and leaped.

I landed easily on the grass and let myself roll down the grassy knoll away from the house. Looking back, I saw that I'd jumped past the glass windows of the large, formal dining room. Two liveried servants were there, but luckily for me, their backs were toward the windows. They were fussing over something in silver platters on sideboards at the back of the room.

I picked myself up and headed down the slope, making sure to steer left to avoid the lights coming from the swimming pool area. The coast looked clear as I headed toward the grove of trees that surrounded the carriage house. The place had only one door and no windows. The large arches, where formerly carriages and horses entered, had been bricked up. The massive, old-fashioned oak door to the carriage house fortunately had a cylindrical modern lock, its shininess indicating that it had been installed fairly recently. I took out a lock-breaking device and fitted its parts against the cylinder. It was then that I heard a voice at my elbow.

"What the hell are you up to?"

I turned, making sure that my back was to the door and hiding the lock-breaking device from view. I faced a man who must have been the "gardener" Pilar had encountered earlier that afternoon. He wore chinos and a wide-brimmed straw hat. I noticed a bulge in the pocket of his frayed cotton jacket that indicated he had a weapon that most gardeners don't need.

"Sorry, old man," I said, "didn't mean to startle you. I just came down here to take a leak. I'm at the party at El Conde Ruiz's, and the one upstairs was occupied." The man looked me up and down suspiciously. He could hardly fail to notice that I wore a tuxedo, and I guess he was afraid of making a wrong move and offending one of El Conde's guests.

Finally he said, begrudgingly, "There's plenty of places in the pool house."

"Would you show me where?" I asked.

He sighed and said, "Come on." The subtext was: these crazy rich people. As we moved away from the carriage house, I noted that he didn't lead the way, he slyly kept to my side. And I also noted that his hand stayed near the bulge in his jacket. I knew that the pool area was visible from all the windows at the back of El Conde's house, and anyone looking this way would be able to see both of us as we moved into the light. I didn't want that.

I stumbled and then muttered a curse. Then I stumbled again, feigning drunkenness. Finally, just on the edge of the light, I lurched and bent over.

"What's wrong mister?" the man said, bending over my doubled up body. I came up hard, my fist against his right jaw. He crumpled to the wet grass, out cold. I took his gun out of his jacket pocket, and then pulled the jacket off him. I ripped the jacket into several long strips. One I rolled up and stuffed into his mouth. With another I bound his wrists and with a third I bound his hands. Then I lifted him and carried him to one of the trees in back of the carriage house. I didn't want him coming to and yelling or trying to stop my search.

Back at the carriage house, I quickly got the lock undone and pushed against the big wooden door. The door made little noise as it swung inward, which meant that it was used regularly. If it hadn't been opened for awhile, the door would have groaned and creaked as it opened. I stepped into the carriage house, pulling the door behind me. I was surrounded by total darkness, the air was silent. I stood still for several seconds, then I switched on my small, powerful flashlight. What I saw was exactly what the place purported to be: a deserted carriage house. Shining the light into all the corners of the room, I saw that the floor was covered with dirt, the walls and stall partitions were crumbling, and cobwebs hung from the rafters. My disappointment was immense.

Just as I was ready to turn off my flashlight and head back to the party, I looked down and changed my mind. Although the floor all around was covered with dirt, a narrow path had been made across the room, so heavily trod the stone floor was almost shiny. I followed the path of exposed floor, which lead to the far end of the carriage house. Here, to the side of, and slightly camouflaged by, a wooden stall, was another door. I knew, from my survey of the outside of the building, that this door didn't lead out, that it had to lead into another room. Slowly, I opened it. What I saw startled me.

I was looking down a broad stairwell. It was fluorescently lit, had freshly painted white walls, and boasted a shiny steel staircase. It appeared that the carriage house was, like Ruiz's mansion, a blend of the "traditional" and the "contemporary." Silently I crept down the wide staircase, unpocketing Wilhelmina as I reached the bottom. I found myself in a sort of reception area. Through glass panels I could see into a room that looked like some sort of laboratory. A white-coated man, who was either a scientist or technician of some sort, sat at a desk at the far end of the room. Another man sat just inside the laboratory, reading a comic book. He wore a blue work shirt, El Grupo's uniform, and there was a high-caliber rifle sitting beside him. Neither man had seen or heard me come into the hall.

I made my way along the glass-paneled wall until I was a few steps from the door to the laboratory—and from the blue-shirted guard.

"Don't move," I yelled, stepping into the doorway. The man in white rose and looked in my direction. The guard whipped around, grabbing his rifle and aiming it at my chest. I fired and hit him right between the eyes. His rifle went off with a loud bang as he hit the floor, then it clattered to the side of the room. The scientist remained motionless as he looked down at his dead companion, whose blood was now running onto the white tile floor of the laboratory.

"Okay," I said, "hands above your head, and don't try anything funny or you'll get what your buddy got." The white-coated man placed his hands where I wanted them, and he glanced involuntarily toward a lighted control panel a few feet to his left. I crossed the room, covering the man with Wilhelmina. I studied the panel. It looked like some sort of two-way warning system, designed to alert someone elsewhere in the building or perhaps in Ruiz's house, if anything went wrong. I wanted to remove the temptation of touching the panel from the scientist.

"Where's the off switch?" I said, pointing at the panel.

"I don't know what you're talking about," the man said.

I cocked Wilhelmina, and he suddenly knew what I was talking about. "To the left," he said, "there's a black lever. Pull it down. That deactivates the system."

"Okay," I said, "if the system doesn't go off when I pull this lever, you're a dead duck." I placed my hand on the black lever.

"No," the man yelled. "There's a switch underneath the console. Turn that." I reached under the console and did just that. The lights on the panel went out.

"Now," I said, looking around at the elaborately-equipped laboratory, "you want to tell me what gives here? What kind of work are you doing?"

"Just engineering research for Mr. Ruiz's construction firm," the man said hastily. "Mr. Ruiz is going to be very upset when he finds out that you're here."

"Yeah," I said, "I'm sure he will be. But I don't get you. I thought that engineers worked on construction, but it looks to me like you're working on destruction here." The blood drained from the man's face. I'd noticed a large blow-up of a diagram on the counter before me. "What, for example," I said, lifting up the gray and white diagram, "is this?"

"It's a . . ." the man stuttered, "it's a plan, the internal plan, for a new bridge."

The blown-up diagram had "TOP SECRET" stenciled across its side, and "Spanish Department of Defense" written on its bottom. I was pretty certain that it was a blow-up of the nuclear plans that had been stolen from General Rodriguez. I guessed that the man beside me was either working on cracking the code or that he'd already done that and was now building a bomb from the plan.

"So the Spanish government's now in the business of building bridges, huh?" I taunted him. He didn't reply but he didn't need to.

"Where's the original for this plan?" I asked. Again he was silent, but his involuntary glance toward a corridor leading off the laboratory betrayed him. I was tired of the man's evasive answers, didn't have time for them. His glance had given me what I needed, and I decided I'd deal with him later, when I had more time. I tied and gagged him, then locked him in a small coat closet at the side of the laboratory. I set a match to the copy of the atomic diagram, then set off down the corridor to look for the original and check out the rest of Ruiz's operation.

The first room I entered gave me all the evidence I needed to convince me that El Conde Ruiz was indeed the head of, or was at least sheltering, El Grupo Febrero. The room contained a set of alphabetically-ordered file cabinets. As I went rapidly through them, I discovered detailed plots and itineraries of all the kidnappings that El Grupo had so far attempted. They contained lists of the personnel, automobiles, weapons and other equipment used in each operation. Precise logs indicated the everyday activities of all of the kidnapping and shooting victims, showing that El Grupo had monitored each man's habits for months before striking. The painstaking and detailed planning of each operation explained the amazing success of El Grupo's plots.

I also found floor plans and detailed notes on the operation of each building El Grupo had bombed, along with lists of the kinds and numbers of bombs they'd used at each sight. There was information about which personnel had completed each mission, and each file contained a report explaining and evaluating the success of each completed strike.

Also, filed under "KGB" I found a log detailing El Grupo's conversations with Nozdrev. From what I could gather, they'd always planned on tricking him, but their motivation for doing so was obscure. Indeed, a peculiarity of all of the files was that the motivations for all their activities were no where discussed in the reports before me. Only the physical details of each operation were recorded.

Also missing from the files was an account of El Grupo's future activities. I supposed these must be kept somewhere else. As were, apparently, the original nuclear plans. I stepped back into the corridor.

The next room I entered was obviously El Grupo's communication center. The place was dark now, indicating that no operations were going on this evening. The room was equipped with an elaborate switchboard, with many microphones. A computerized map of Spain above the switchboard was apparently used for monitoring the locations of El Grupo's various operatives. It was here, no doubt, that headquarters communicated with their men in the field. I thought back to the radio in the truck of the men at Maria's. Also, to one side of the room, was a glass-enclosed, soundproof recording studio; it was here that El Grupo made their revolutionary "communiques." I marveled at the sophistication of the whole operation.

The next room I entered made my eyes widen in

amazement. Here I found an enormous atomic
stockpile. In an adjoining room was the equipment
necessary to build the collection of bombs. In a
safe here, which I cracked fairly easily, I at last located the original atomic diagrams that General
Rodriguez had been carrying and also the plans
concerning the movements of the Spanish army
and airforce that had been stolen from him. Even
more ominous, however, were the other contents of
the safe. It contained many atomic formulas, and
from the stockpiles it was obvious that these had
already been used. El Conde Ruiz and El Grupo
would have had to have worked several years to
build up the weapons in this room, and these plans
indicated that someone, possibly the man I'd just
been with, had already found the secret of nuclear
fission on his own. El Grupo had no doubt been
working to put into effect the plan they'd stolen
from Rodriguez, but they didn't really need it. The
group already had all the weapons they needed to
blow up half the people on the face of the earth.
They certainly could wreak havoc in any country
or countries they chose to attack. This thing was
bigger, much bigger than we'd ever imagined.

Pocketing Rodriguez's and the other nuclear
plans, I stepped back into the corridor. Glancing at
my watch, I saw that I had fifteen minutes to make
it out of here and get back to the mansion. I went
to the final room at the end of the corridor and
opened the door. The room I entered looked like
an extension of Ruiz's house: white carpet, a white
sofa, elegant chrome and glass tables, even an expensive abstract painting on the wall. A stereo
played one of Beethoven's quartets, and a man was

sitting on the white sofa.

He was General Rodriguez, the latest kidnap
victim of El Grupo, the man who had set in motion
my mission to Spain. Rodriguez looked up at me as
I entered, obviously startled. He rose, and momentarily cowered against the wall, apparently frightened of me. Looking down, I realized that I still
had Wilhelmina in my hand, and that the gun
pointed at him. I aimed toward the floor.

The tall, gray-haired man before me was obviously edgy, but he retained his military bearing
and he looked to be in pretty good health, for a
man who'd been locked up for the last week. He
was still wearing the uniform he'd been kidnapped in.

"General Rodriguez," I said.

"Yes. Who are you?"

"I've come to help you, from Spanish Intelligence."

"I never expected you to make it," he said, in a
low voice. "How did you find me?"

"That's too long a story to go into now," I said.
"The important thing is that I'm here. What we've
got to do now is get you out." Rodriguez nodded.
"Are you all right?" I said, "Physically?"

"I'm okay," he said, in a nervous voice. "They
haven't treated me too badly."

"No," I said, glancing around the fancy room.
"I didn't expect them to keep you in such luxurious
quarters."

"They haven't treated me badly," he repeated.

"They didn't torture you to make that tape?" I
asked, remembering the broken voice I'd heard on
the communique at the beginning of Rodriguez's
"trial."

He lowered his head. "Ah, yes, they did torture me for that," he said tonelessly. "But afterward they brought me here. I got the feeling that they were saving me for some spectacular kind of ending, and I shudder to think what that may be."

"Well," I said, "it won't be anything now. Let's get out of here."

"What about the guards?" Rodriguez asked. "How did you get in?"

"I shot one guard."

"Ah."

"Are there others?"

"Yes," Rodriguez said, nervously glancing at a clock on the wall. "A second guard comes on duty at nine-thirty." The clock read 9:35. "We'll have to get by him." I cursed.

"What about that door?" I said, indicating a door at the side of the room. "Is it another exit?"

"Yes, but I don't know where it leads. One of the men sometimes enters there."

"El Conde Ruiz?"

"Yes," Rodriguez said flatly, "El Conde Ruiz."

"He's the head of El Grupo Febrero?"

"As far as I can figure out, yes. The others take their orders from him. Why don't you try the door, Mr. . . ."

I moved to the door, which was locked. General Rodriguez was behind me.

"I think Ruiz sometimes pushes this button before he goes out," Rodriguez said, moving his hand to a lighted knob to the left of the door.

"No, dammit," I yelled, "that's probably a signaling device!" But it was too late. Rodriguez had already pressed the button.

"I'm sorry," he said, jumping back, "I thought it might be used to unlock the door."

I silently cursed, but said aloud, "Well, it can't be helped now." I jiggled the door. "And it didn't unlock the door. But I've got a lock breaker, which should open it up." I pulled the device out of my pocket and fitted it to the cylindrical lock, which was just like the lock on the carriage house door. I swirled the lock.

"Okay, that's enough Mr. Carter," Rodriguez said. His voice was suddenly strong and authoritative, and he had a gun jammed into my back. He took Wilhelmina out of my hand. "Now put your hands against the wall," he said, "and don't move."

I should have guessed before: the elegantly furnished sitting room, the music, the lack of any evidence of torture and Rodriguez's general fitness despite his captivity. All pointed to the obvious: General Rodriguez had engineered his own kidnapping, no doubt in collaboration with Ruiz. Now I understood one of the puzzles of the case, why Rodriguez had notified no one the day he was kidnapped that he would be transporting top-secret documents. Of course he hadn't, because a superior might have stopped him and foiled his and El Grupo's clever "kidnap" plan.

"So you kidnapped yourself, huh?" I said.

"You might put it that way."

"Quite a hoax."

"Thank you."

"And I suppose that the button you pressed really is a signaling device?"

"That's correct, Mr. Carter. El Conde Ruiz will

be joining us as soon as he can leave his guests. In the meantime, some of his boys will be coming down to help me with you. You've already caused us too much trouble."

"Can't blame me for trying."

"Ah, but we do blame you, Mr. Carter. You've interrupted our plans on a number of occasions, and I'm sure El Conde and I will think of some appropriate way of dealing with you. Which may not be very pleasant." Rodriguez laughed, a short sadistic laugh. I could just imagine what his and Ruiz's way of dealing with me would be. Slow torture and death no doubt. I had to act before Ruiz's boys arrived, but what was I to do with Rodriguez's gun jammed into my back? I only hoped that Pilar could manage to do something when I failed to appear at dinner.

The Beethoven quartet ended. I felt the pressure of the gun in my back let up, and I heard Rodriguez moving away from me.

"Just going to change the tape," he said. "I wouldn't want to deprive you of music, would I? El Conde tells me you're quite fond of culture. But remember that my gun is aimed at your spinal cord. If you make one move you'll be dead. Or perhaps—and this might even be more amusing than your actual death—I could paralyze you." Again he laughed. The man really was a sadistic bastard. I could well imagine who had thought up the mad schemes of torture El Grupo had practiced.

I heard the click of a cartridge being removed from a tape deck. I knew that Rodriguez's eyes, if only for a couple of seconds, would be on selecting and putting in a new tape. I hoped that those seconds were now. I threw myself away from the wall, and I heard a bullet whiz past me. But Rodriguez's timing was, as I'd hoped, a fraction of a second late. His bullet sunk into the wall I'd been standing against. I made my way toward him, deliberately zig-zagging to throw his aim off balance. His second bullet burned a hole in the sleeve of my tuxedo, but it just missed my flesh.

I was upon him now, and I threw myself against his tall, stocky body. With my left hand I grasped his gun arm. His right arm came down, moving the gun close to my face. But just as he fired, I managed to jerk both our arms up, and the bullet blasted into the ceiling above us. Then I jabbed hard into the side of his ribs with my free hand. The impact of the blow apparently weakened him for a second, and I took the opportunity to dig my fingers as hard into the flesh of Rodriguez's wrist as I could. The gun flew out of his hand into a corner of the room.

We loosened our grips on one another and stood there for a second looking into each others' eyes. Rodriguez's were dark and small and hard, like those of a vicious animal unexpectedly crossed. He came at me, aiming a punch at my mouth. But I blocked with my left and sunk my right fist into his exposed gut. He staggered backwards, bellowing. From a stand at the side of the room, he pulled out an old-fashioned, military saber.

"I'll kill you, Carter," Rodriguez roared as he approached me. He swung the saber from left to right, aiming at my neck. I ducked just in time to miss the sharp blade by a fraction of an inch. Rodriguez swiftly aimed again, this time bringing

the saber up vertically between my legs. I jumped
backwards just in time. Had he hit, he would have
sliced me in two, beginning at my crotch.

Before he had a chance to aim again, I flexed my
right forearm and Hugo slipped into my hand.
Rodriguez swung the saber, going again for my
head. I ducked and could feel the rush of air the
swing created against the back of my neck.
Rodriguez may even have sliced off a hair or two
that time. Still crouched, I sent the stiletto sailing
toward Rodriguez, and it landed where I wanted it:
in the arm that held the saber. Blood jetted from
Rodriguez's forearm as the stiletto hit, and the
saber fell at his feet. I rushed to him and yanked
Hugo out of his arm before he had a chance to grab
the stiletto himself. He howled with pain, then he
stood still, holding his wounded arm with his other
hand. I guess he didn't want another blow from
Hugo. I stood before the General, bringing the
stiletto close to his face.

"All right, Rodriguez," I said, "enough fun and
games. If you don't want your face carved up, tell
me which way Ruiz's boys will be coming from." I
wanted to try to get out the other exit. But
Rodriguez hesitated. Blood had drained from his
face and his eyes were frightened holes, but he remained silent.

"Tell," I said, inching the stiletto closer to his
face. Then I felt a blow like that of a sledgehammer
against the back of my head. The impact of the
blow sent me lurching forward and sent the tip of
the stiletto into Rodriguez's face, from just below
his eye to his jaw. The trail of cut flesh and blood
was the last thing I saw before I passed out.

Chapter Eleven

I felt something cold and hard beneath my body. My head ached. In the distance I could hear muffled voices, but I couldn't make out their words. Slowly, I opened my eyes. I was staring up at an enormous domed ceiling, maybe five hundred feet above me. Fluorescent tubing hung down from steel grids near its top. I lifted my head. Several feet in front of me I saw a group of men in blue workshirts talking. To my left there was another group. I lowered my head and closed my eyes.

"He's awake," I heard one of the men say.

"I saw him move," said another. Footsteps moved toward me.

"Hey, Mister," a voice said. "Wake up." I decided it wasn't going to do me any good to play possum. Might as well face the music now as later. I felt for Wilhelmina and Hugo, but of course, they were both gone. I opened my eyes. I was looking up into the dark faces of a group of maybe a dozen or so Spanish men. They stood in a circle now, surrounding me. Other men stood behind them. So this was how it was going to end.

"You all right?" said one of the men.

"As well as can be expected, considering the blow you guys gave me."

"No, no you've got it all wrong, Mister." I looked at the speaker. I recognized him as Esteban, one of the men whose photographs I'd picked up this afternoon. Looking around at the faces glowering above me, I also picked out the three other men whose families I'd talked to earlier that day.

"Yeah, I've got it all wrong, Esteban," I said cynically.

"How'd you know my name," Esteban asked suspiciously.

"That's a long story," I said. "How long have you had me here?" Was it hours, days, a week?

"You've been here about two hours," said a tall man with long hair and a mustache. "What are you doing here?"

"You tell me."

"Look," he said, "we didn't have anything to do with knocking you out. You had that blow on your head when they sent you down here."

"Who is they?" I asked.

"Ruiz's men."

"And who the hell are you?" The men all laughed at this question. "And what's so funny?" I asked irritably.

"We don't have anything to do with Ruiz," said the man in the mustache, "except that we're his prisoners."

"What?" I sat up straight. Were they putting me on?

"Here, let me help you," said one man as I rose to my feet, weaving a bit. "I'm a doctor." The head wound had made me dizzy.

"You're Ruiz's prisoners?" I asked incredulously.

"Yeah, man, just like you." It was the tall man with the mustache. He seemed to be the group's spokesman. I didn't understand what game was going on.

"But you are El Grupo," I said.

"No!" It was a shout, with practically every man in the room joining in, loud and angry. Yet I'd seen the photographs of some of them and knew that they were with El Grupo Febrero, or at least had been at one point. I wondered, briefly, if my head wound was making me hallucinate.

"We don't have any connection with that gang of terrorists," said the men's leader.

"No?"

"No."

"So what are you doing here?"

"Like I said, man, we're prisoners. Ruiz kidnapped us. What are *you* doing here?"

"He kidnapped you?"

"Yeah."

"All of you?" It was hard to believe.

"Yeah, all of us. There are twenty-three of us all together, not counting one guy Ruiz killed, and one guy he apparently missed."

"Pedro Salas?" I asked.

"Yes. How did you know about Pedro?"

"Maybe the man's a spy of Ruiz's," came a shout from the back of the group.

"That it?" asked the man in the mustache. "I hope not, because if you are, we'll kill you. There isn't anything Ruiz can do to us in return now, except kill us. And maybe some of us would rather die than stay cooped up in here for much longer."

"I was a friend of Maria's, Pedro's sister," I said. "She asked me to look for Pedro. He was in hiding."

"Did you find him?"

"I found him all right. Dead."

"Christ," said Esteban, "he was a friend of mine. I think somehow Pedro knew they were after us all. I guess they were trying to hunt him down too, and they couldn't capture him, like they had us, so they killed him."

"You mean you boys didn't?" I asked. Esteban came with his fist toward my face, calling me a bastard, but the other men restrained him.

"We don't kill innocent people," said the man with the mustache.

"Tell me about it," I said.

"Why should we trust you? How do we know you're not on Ruiz's side?"

"Would he have clobbered me over the head and put me in here with you, who claim to be his prisoners, if I was working with him?"

"You've got a point there. Okay, what do we have to lose?" The man exchanged looks with several of his friends and they all nodded for him to go ahead. The story I then heard, told to me by the man in the mustache, whose name was Garcia, was one of the strangest tales I'd ever heard. Yet I believed it: it somehow seemed to match up with other stories I'd heard from these men's wives and families, from Dona Pretiosa, and above all from Maria. As Garcia spoke, his friends often interrupted him, adding their own clarifications and explanations to his words, but basically his story boiled down to this:

All of the men in the room with me had been, at one point in their lives, members of a study group at the University in Barcelona. The university group was, indeed, called "El Grupo Febrero." The group had been opposed to the policies of the former government of Spain, and for that reason had been secret. Their politics, however, had been more on a theoretical than on a practical level. They had worked against the government mainly by writing and printing pamphlets and leaflets which criticized the repression and the economic backwardness of the Franco regime. The group hadn't even been able to hold public meetings for fear of being imprisoned.

Several years ago, when democracy had suddenly flowered in Spain, the group had disbanded. There was no more reason to print El Grupo's leaflets and pamphlets, and besides, most of the men, by this time, had graduated from college and were more concerned with their new careers and families than with any further radical political activities. They now numbered among themselves three doctors, two lawyers, an actor, two businessmen, and men who practiced a variety of other occupations. In short, the men surrounding me could just about serve as a representative cross-section of young, educated professionals.

A few of the men had maintained their friendships over the last few years, but most of the men of El Grupo Febrero had seen each other for the first time in several years when they'd been brought together here.

Slightly less than two months ago, each of the men here had been abducted by three men, "big, rough-looking men in work shirts," Garcia said, which corresponded to the men I'd encountered from—well, the other "El Grupo." Some of the men had been grabbed as they came home from work, others had been taken from their apartments (if they lived alone), one man had even been stopped when he was out bicycling. They had all been blindfolded, given some kind of drug, and driven to an unknown destination. When they had awakened, they had found themselves in the room where we now were. No one had left the room since that day.

When the men had first arrived here, they could make no sense of their predicament. After they'd talked and pieced together their identical kidnappings and finally realized that what they all had in common was that they had all once been members of "El Grupo Febrero" in college, they were still puzzled about why they had been brought here. For several days they were in suspense and came up with every conjecture in the world: that they had been brought here by a homocidal maniac; that they were being recruited by the government secret service; that a fascistic regime had again returned to power. One man, a science-fiction buff, even argued that, because of the futuristic design of the chamber we were in, they had been captured by men from outer space.

I looked around the chamber. It certainly did look like a space ship or something. I was convinced, however, that it was in fact located deep in the bowels of Ruiz's estate, probably below the un-

derground rooms I'd been in earlier. It was a large
cylinder-shaped room with steel walls and very
high ceilings. Steel bunk beds, in orderly rows,
lined one side of the chamber. On the other side
there were rows of sinks and showers and toilets—
like in a prison or a military barracks. In the center
of the room were a number of tables, and chairs,
and two television sets with extra large screens.
There were also a number of exercise machines.

Garcia pointed out to me two large openings in
the ceiling. He said that long cylinders descended
from these. One cylinder, like a modernized ver-
sion of a dumb waiter, sent the men three hot meals
a day. The men had soon learned that if they
placed their leftovers and dirty dishes in the
cylinder, they would be whisked away as the
cylinder ascended back into the ceiling. The other
cylinder, smaller than the first, sent down clean
and took back soiled laundry: towels, the uniform
clothes the men were wearing (blue work shirts,
jeans, sweat socks), and bedclothes.

For the first few days after the men arrived here,
they saw no one else. They screamed and shouted
for someone to come to them, but no one had.
Then one evening a man appeared on the balcony.
They pointed out a steel balcony, high above our
heads, which was encased in what was no doubt
bullet-proof glass. The man told them that he was
El Conde Ruiz and announced that he had re-
assembled "El Grupo Febrero" and was pleased to
have them on his team. Not one of the men had
ever seen Ruiz before, although one man did remember that Ruiz had once been a high government official. That night Ruiz read to the men an

account of the first kidnapping performed by "El Grupo Febrero" and ironically congratulated them on "the good job." The men, of course, had yelled and cursed at Ruiz, but he hadn't responded to them. After he left, the two television screens suddenly came on, broadcasting television accounts of El Grupo Febrero's bloody activities.

This pattern continued. The men neither heard nor saw any people except Ruiz. Every few days he came in and read to them from newspaper accounts of El Grupo Febrero's activities. At first they yelled up at him—pleas, questions, threats, curses—but when they realized that Ruiz was never going to respond to them they quit trying. The television sets were obviously remote-controlled and came on only to broadcast program and newscasts about El Grupo Febrero.

As the weeks passed, the men's rage and frustration grew daily. The worst was, as it was no doubt intended to be, when they had to listen to the lists of crimes committed in their names. Many men in the chamber had periodically thought of committing suicide, either individually or collectively, but they had worked out a pact among themselves to protect one another—both physically and mentally —and so far they had managed to keep bodies and souls alive. When they'd arrived their first thoughts had turned to escape, of course. But when they checked out the room, they discovered that it was virtually escape-proof. Once, one of the men had tried to climb up the cylinder that brought their food. But after he'd climbed up a certain distance the cylinder was jerked up into its hole with such force that the man fell and severely strained his back. This led them to believe that they were monitored at virtually all times, and they were fairly certain that the many perforations in the domed ceiling contained microphones and video cameras.

The men, were, at least, well fed, and they spent their days exercising, inventing all kinds of verbal and physical games, and talking. The most popular topics of conversation were their families, their jobs, and speculations on El Conde Ruiz's motives.

Except for El Conde, I was the first person the men had seen in almost two months. "And how did I get down here?" I asked. "There doesn't seem to be a staircase." Garcia pointed to another hole in the ceiling, near the balcony. Apparently a chute opened out of that. I'd come sliding down the chute; then it had been immediately pulled back up.

Garcia and the other men were full of speculations about what Ruiz was planning to do with them: kill them? free them? hold them here forever? The men were certain of two things, however. One, Ruiz and company were obviously using the name of "El Grupo Febrero" as a cover for their own bloody activities—activities which were not really "revolutionary" at all. And two, Ruiz was a madman. I had to agree with them on both accounts. Ruiz was, clearly, in some sense, completely out of his mind. Yet he was crazy like a fox. Leaving aside value judgements for a moment, one couldn't help but be impressed by the cleverness of Ruiz's cover, and the brilliant organization of his campaign. Ruiz was, unfortunately for us and for the people of Spain, some kind of genius. The diabolical kind. I wondered what his plans were for the men here and what his plans for me were. And I wondered why he was doing what he was doing. Was Ruiz just power mad or was there something more behind his campaign of terror?

I didn't have to wait long for some answers to my questions. About an hour after I awoke and found myself surrounded by the captured men, a light came on in the balcony. El Conde Ruiz appeared above us. He'd changed out of his tuxedo into a full-dress Spanish military uniform, heavily decorated with ribbons and medals. He tapped on a microphone to announce himself, and we all quit talking and looked up at him. There was complete silence in the chamber as he cleared his throat and began speaking.

"Good evening, gentlemen," he said, flashing his white teeth. "Tonight I want to thank you all for working with me all these weeks. You've helped to make my operation a splendid success merely by your presence here." There was malicious and taunting irony in Ruiz's tone and the amplification of his voice by the microphone system made his voice eerie—like some larger-than-life phantom.

"I should tell you gentlemen," Ruiz continued, "that your new companion is Mr. Nick Carter, an agent of the American government. Mr. Carter has been trying—none too successfully—" (and here Ruiz let out a short, dry laugh) "to foil my activities. I wouldn't take to kindly to Mr. Carter if I were you gentlemen. He's not to be trusted." I turned my head and glanced about me. The men were looking at me accusingly. I hoped only because I hadn't told them who I was.

"Now, gentlemen," Ruiz said, "after tonight I'm afraid I will no longer require your services." The men looked at one another questioningly. I was afraid they had every reason to fear the worst. "Before you gentlemen, uh, leave, I wish to tell you what has been happening in Spain these last few months that you've been confined, and why I brought you here.

"I want to begin by telling you about my father, the late El Conde Ruiz, whose title I've proudly inherited. My father was a great man, a noble and a patriotic man. He fought bravely and loyally with Generalissimo Franco during the Spanish Civil War that tore our country asunder. He fought against the anarchistic and socialistic elements of his day. These villains were men who, not unlike yourselves gentlemen, believed that the old order had to be torn down, that the old ideals of courage and power and control should be spit upon. My father fought for what he believed in, and he was shot down, in cold blood, and in the back, by a group of vicious, communistic swine. When my father died, I said to myself that I would one day wipe your kind from the earth forever." The men exchanged nervous glances.

"All through my youth," Ruiz said, "I studied the teachings of the church and of the Franco state in order to be a man like my father. I joined the youth group of Franco's regime and distinguished myself there. But when I went to university, I was suddenly confronted with trouble-making students —and teachers. These people ridiculed men like my father, who had died a heroic death. These people felt that men like my father should be replaced in power by the poor, the worthless, the ne'er-do-wells who always want something for nothing. The students in my day, as in yours, had their sentimental ideas about 'justice' and 'liberty.' But why, I ask you, should we have justice for men who contribute nothing to society and liberty for those who are tearing down the pillars of society?

"After I left college, I worked my way up in the government serving the regime I believed in with all my heart, the regime my father had died for. I worked hard because I knew that some day I would have the chance to rule this country myself and would be able to rid it of all the undesirable elements. I made my way steadily and rapidly to the inner circles of the regime, and I gathered around me a group of influential governmental and army leaders.

"Then our great leader died, and immediately the jackals rushed in to pick over his corpse, to slander him and all he'd done for the country. And the King entered, at first speaking softly, not quite betraying his silly 'principles.' But then, publicly, he turned against the man who had brought him out of exile, the man who had restored him to his throne. This King began desecrating the memory of the leader that I still honored. The King turned out to be a wolf in sheep's clothing after all. Or rather, a sheep in wolf's clothing. Pretending to be a strong leader, the King showed himself weak by caving in to the demands of the bleeding-heart liberals. He brought with him into government men who were distinguished only by their weakness, men who in the former regime would have been spit upon, or imprisoned. They prattled on about 'democracy.' But I ask you, gentlemen, what is democracy except the weak will of the lowest and most stupid members of society?

"This mediocrity is what my father, and later I, had fought against all our lives. But I decided to stay within the government. I hoped that I could push the ideals I believed in, and that the King would some day be forced to come around. I was confident I could overpower these weak new government men."

Ruiz's voice had reached a pitch of anger and shrillness. I recalled a film I'd seen, *Triumph of the Will*, about the Nazis, in which Hitler had given a long speech. In Ruiz, I saw the same self-righteousness, the same wounded fury, the same mad rhetoric that I'd seen in Hitler. Fortunately for all of us, Hitler hadn't had any nuclear weapons; unfortunately Ruiz did.

"Not only did the government not give me a chance to put my ideas in action," Ruiz shouted, "but the King and his weak cohorts ridiculed those ideas. Then they decided to get rid of me—me, El Conde Ruiz, whose lineage can be traced back to the twelfth century and whose family had loyally served this government during times of crisis for years. And so they sacked me, the King and his men, cast me off like an old dog whose time had passed.

"That was their mistake, gentlemen. I left the government politely, not giving them the satisfaction of knowing my real feelings about them. I hated them, and I vowed that I would revenge myself on these men. I vowed that I would use their own methods against them. They wanted 'democracy'? Very well. I would show them what happens when you let the weakest and most contemptible elements of the populace take part in politics. They wanted 'freedom' for even the lowliest of men. Very well. I would show them what happens when they let the anarchistic elements have their freedom. I would show them that their democracy and the freedom they granted to men like you would destroy the government and the foundations of our society.

"That's where you come in, gentlemen." Ruiz looked down on the heads of the men assembled below him. "I used to work in the information department in the government. I kept tabs on, and had under surveillance by government agents, men like yourselves, organizations like 'El Grupo Febrero.' The new government ordered my department to destroy the records we'd been keeping for years.

"Only I fooled them. I knew that a time would come when you people would strike again. I waited. I built up my own force of men, men who, like myself, were disillusioned with the King and his new government. I bided my time. I built up my arsenal and my information network. And then I struck. I struck to prove to the government and to the people of Spain that this silly 'democracy' and 'freedom' could not preserve our country from harm. I set out to prove that even a small, weak group like yourselves, El Grupo Febrero, could set the government into disarray and destroy the country's morale. You see, gentlemen, I'd taken your names with me when I left the information service, knowing that some day I'd need you.

"Now," Ruiz continued, "the seeds of my plan are bearing fruit, thanks to you, El Grupo Febrero." Ruiz laughed a long, mad laugh. "All over Spain people are growing disenchanted with the ability of the present government to preserve order. They realize, more and more, what this 'democracy' has led to: anarchy, attacks against their families and loved ones, a reign of terror!"

Ruiz's logic and argument were impeccable except for one point: He was himself creating the disorder he claimed to be working so fervently against; the reign of terror was his own.

"And so, gentlemen," Ruiz concluded, "I want to thank you again. Soon my men and I will rid this country of its weak King. The people will follow us, thanks to you. At this point our plan is bound to succeed; no one can stop us." Ruiz looked down at me to emphasize this last point. "I will require your services no more after tonight, gentlemen. I bid you a final farewell."

Ruiz gave a military salute, then stepped off the balcony, out of sight. The lights in his glass booth went out. I shook my head and exchanged looks with the men whose faces betrayed their deep dismay. I think everyone there knew exactly what Ruiz meant by bidding us a "final farewell." If they didn't they found out almost immediately. As soon as Ruiz disappeared, a hissing sound began. The hissing came from the floor vents of the chamber.

"What's that noise?" asked a man in a frightened voice. I was pretty sure that the hissing meant that we were being gassed. The hissing increased in volume as the gas was shot into the chamber under force of a great deal of pressure.

"Quick," I yelled, "we're being gassed. Strip the blankets and sheets off the beds and put them over the air ducts on the floor." We all ran to the side of the room and ferociously began stripping the beds. We threw the heavy blankets and also the sheets over the ducts, trying to impede the flow of the gas. But it was no use. The pressure forcing the gas into the room was too great to be stopped. Despite our best efforts, gas continued seeping into the chamber. It permeated the air around our heads. Men were beginning to cough and choke. They were running every which way in the room, trying to escape the onslaught of the gas. We were going to die like trapped rats.

"Cover your faces with wet cloths," yelled one of the men, a doctor. I knew the gas was too strong for that, that the wet cloths weren't going to stop anything, but immediately there was a run on the sinks and showers and even the toilets, and men covered their faces with wet towels, washclothes, shirts. As they wandered about the room, cloths on heads, the place looked like some ghastly science fiction set filled with faceless men. It was a chilling vision.

And the wet cloths didn't do any good. Men were now gasping for breath and moaning from pain. I threw myself to the cold steel floor, hoping that the gas would rise rapidly to the ceiling of the chamber. I held my breath for long periods of time, and then took sharp, small gasps of air into my lungs.

I saw that some of the men had already collapsed onto the floor, and I wondered if they were dead. One of the men sprawled out, motionless, was

Miguel, whose wife and children I'd talked to that afternoon. I thought of them and remembered bitterly predicting that if Miguel ever came home to his wife and kids it would be in a coffin. Only I hadn't guessed that the method would be the same one used by Hitler against the Jews.

More and more men had fallen to the floor and were writhing there in pain. They were like the figures of the damned out of Dante. Their cries pierced the air. This was really *Godderdamurung* time. Then I caught my first whiff of the gas and felt my body go sick and queasy as it entered my lungs. I held my breath again. I could tell from the smell of the gas that it wasn't cyanide, as I'd expected. But to know it wasn't cyanide wasn't much of a comfort. There are lots of gasses that can kill men besides cyanide, and it was a pretty safe bet to say that Ruiz and his men had used one of them. I guessed we all had maybe another ten minutes.

Already, most of the twenty-three men were sprawled on the floor, motionless. I wasn't so much concerned for my own life; that's the risk you run if you're an agent. The odds are, sooner or later, that you're probably going to get it. Few agents live to a ripe old age. But these men were different, merely pawns in Ruiz's game. They were innocent of any crime except the crime of idealism, which had apparently become the most heinous crime of all in Ruiz's twisted imagination. I thought of the men's families and the pain Ruiz was causing them, and I thought of all the men he'd killed in bombings and kidnappings and the people he might well kill with his nuclear weapons. What made a man like Ruiz—rich, cultured, handsome, titled—crave power so much that he would stop at nothing to get it? I think I never wanted to kill a man as badly as I wanted to kill Ruiz.

As I opened my eyes the gas burned them. The silence of the chamber was total now. All of the previously writhing and running and clawing bodies were stilled. It was like a freeze frame in a movie. All motion had been arrested. Apparently I was the last man in the room still conscious. I'd been able to hold out against the gas longer than the others because of my training for situations just like this. But training can control the human organism only up to a certain point. I wouldn't be able to hold out much longer. It felt like I had daggers stabbing into my lungs, urging me to take in some air.

I took a breath. I felt the acrid gas enter my nostrils, and then my lungs. The sensation was that my body was dissolving. My last thought was of Pilar: Where was she? Why hadn't she rescued me? Could I have been right about her after all? Was she a counter agent?

And then I went under.

Chapter Twelve

"Nick . . . Nick?" I heard Pilar's low voice. Had she rescued me after all? I opened my eyes and looked up into her beautiful face, which was now taut with worry. "Nick, I thought you'd never wake up," she said. She bent her head down and kissed my lips. I looked around. We were in an unfamiliar and very strange room. One of the room's yellow stucco walls was oddly curved, and there were no windows and only one door. The place was bare except for a television set in an alcove on one wall. I was lying on my side on a tile floor, and I realized that my hands were tied, with thick ropes, behind my back. Pilar's hands were also bound at the wrist. A piece of music, which sounded vaguely familiar, sounded from somewhere in the distance.

"Where are we?" I asked. "What happened?"

"I don't know. I woke up . . ." Pilar shrugged. "I don't know how long ago. It seems like I've been here for hours and hours, just sitting here."

"That music," I said, "sounds awfully familiar." I could now make out the symphonic orchestration and the voice of a soprano singing in German.

"They've been playing it since I woke up.

They've been playing the same passage over and over again," Pilar said. Suddenly it came to me. The music was Isolde's final aria, her lament for her dead lover, in Wagner's opera, *Tristan and Isolde*. I told Pilar.

"Of course, you're right," she said, "I should have recognized it myself. It's beautiful music, but I wish they'd shut it off. I'm tired of hearing the same thing again and again."

But the aria kept repeating itself as Pilar and I exchanged stories. I told her about my exploration of Ruiz's underground headquarters; about his atomic stockpile; about General Rodriguez's treachery; about the men the two were holding prisoners; and about Ruiz's speech followed by the nightmarish experience in his torture chamber.

"I guess I was wrong about the gas being poisoned," I observed. "It was only strong enough to knock me out for awhile. But there's no doubt we were *meant* to think the gas was poisonous—one of Ruiz's and Rodriguez's sadistic little games."

"I guess I got off luckier," Pilar said, "they drugged me with a needle." She showed me the mark on her right forearm.

While I had been underground, Pilar had had her own troubles. When Ruiz's Bach concert had ended, she'd noticed, of course, that I hadn't returned. She'd tried to decide what to do, whether to go through dinner and hope that Ruiz didn't note my absence, or whether to excuse herself from dinner as convincingly as she could and try to find me. It turned out, however, that the decision hadn't been Pilar's to make. As she and Ruiz left the music room, the bulging-eyed butler had approached her and told her she was wanted on the phone. Thinking the call might be from me, or possibly from Lorca, Pilar had gone upstairs to take it in her bedroom. There, however, she'd been greeted by a group of Ruiz's henchmen. They'd tied her up and gagged her. They stood guard in her bedroom. About an hour and a half later, apparently after he'd finished dinner and bid his other guests goodnight, El Conde Ruiz had come to Pilar. He'd sent the guards out of the room, and had removed the gag from her mouth. Ruiz made it clear to Pilar that he'd suspected she was an agent for some time, and that he was aware she was in his house to spy on him. Then Ruiz had treated her to a political harangue very much like the one I'd heard in the chamber.

In addition, Ruiz had taunted Pilar about her "weak-willed, liberal" husband and about her "relationship" with "that interfering swine, Nick Carter." Ruiz had gone into a diatribe about Pilar's refusal to marry him, and told her that from now on she would be completely in his power. At one point during their interview Pilar had feared that Ruiz would rape her right then and there—out of vengeance and because of his long-suppressed desire for the woman he now held captive. But Ruiz had spared her that.

"Ruiz always remains a gentleman," Pilar noted sarcastically.

When Pilar had asked Ruiz what he'd done with me, he'd merely replied that both of us would get what was coming to us, and then he'd left the room. About an hour later a man in a white coat had come into Pilar's bedroom (the same white-coated man I'd locked up in the closet?), and he'd given her the shot that had knocked her out. When she woke up she was here beside me.

I wondered why Ruiz had brought Pilar and me back together. And I wondered where we were. If we were still on Ruiz's estate, why hadn't Lorca sent in a team of men to search the place like he'd promised? Surely, it must be morning already.

I noticed that the Wagner music in the distance had stopped. Abruptly the television in the alcove came on. This t.v., like the ones in the chamber, was obviously triggered by some remote control device. The face of General Rodriguez filled the t.v. screen. Pilar gasped. The General was being interviewed by an international panel of journalists about his "escape" from El Grupo earlier this morning. (This at least gave us some idea of the amount of time we'd passed in captivity.) The distinguished journalists were obviously awed by the General; one savant described him as "our latest national" hero, and the others seemed to agree with this assessment. Rodriguez described his stoicism and his refusal to break down during his "captivity." In answer to a question about what tortures he'd undergone, Rodriguez pointed to the long red cut down the side of his face, the cut I'd given him last night, as an example of El Grupo Febrero's "sadistic methods."

In the second segment of this "News Special" a distinguished, gray-haired commentator announced that we'd now be looking at exclusive footage, which the station had just received, of the site of General Rodriguez's "captivity." We'd also hear about Rodriguez's "amazingly heroic" mission of this afternoon. Pilar and I looked at one another and raised our eyebrows. What could this amazingly heroic mission possibly be?

The scene switched to a man in a trench coat holding a microphone. He was standing in a field near what looked to be a bombed-out hacienda. In the background men in army uniforms were lifting charred corpses out of the rubble and placing them on stretchers. The commentator explained, in an unctuous voice, that this was the hideaway, to the south of Barcelona, where General Rodriguez had spent his agonizing and terror-filled week as a prisoner of El Grupo Febrero.

"The bodies you see in the background here," the man announced gleefully, "are the remains of the villains who kidnapped and tried to kill General Rodriguez."

The commentator described, in melodramatic detail, how General Rodriguez, after escaping from his captors, had then returned to the hacienda, leading a battalion of army officers. The army men had laid siege to the building. When the revolutionaries inside had refused to surrender, Rodriguez had ordered his men to bomb the place. El Grupo's "headquarters" had been destroyed. Along with the men inside.

I knew who the men inside the hacienda had been, and I also knew why they hadn't come out of the building and why they had "refused" to surrender. They couldn't surrender because they were still unconscious from the gas that Ruiz had pumped into their lungs. I knew that those corpses belonged to Garcia and Esteban and the other men

I'd been with in Ruiz's chamber. Ruiz and Rodriguez had transported the men they'd kidnapped to this hacienda to make them sitting ducks. This whole newscast was a total outrage. I couldn't believe that Ruiz and Rodriguez were getting away with their hypocritical and lying scheme, but they apparently were. I glanced at Pilar. Tears were rolling down her cheeks. I took her hand.

"I can't believe I knew Juan Ruiz all those years," Pilar said softly, "and that I never even suspected the depths of the man's madness."

The t.v. program switched back to the grayhaired commentator in the studio. He concluded the broadcast by saying that a major arm of the terrorist organization had been felled today, thanks to the heroism of General Rodriguez. But the government believed that there were still members of El Grupo Febrero at large. The government feared that these anarchists would now strike again in retaliation for their colleagues' deaths. With that the television clicked off.

Ah, yes, "El Grupo Febrero" would strike again all right! Before Pilar and I had a chance to discuss these horrifying new events, these lies that Ruiz and Rodriguez had created and that the media was accepting, the door opened. El Conde Ruiz, wearing white tie and tails, stepped into the room. Ruiz smiled at us, the sickly-sweet smile of the victor. Ruiz had come to boast and he was quick and to the point. First he gloated over the success of pulling off Rodriguez's "escape" and his "heroic return," as Ruiz mockingly put it. Then Ruiz outlined his future plans. The King, whom Ruiz so hated, and the government's entire cabinet, would die tonight, Ruiz assured us. Naturally, a new communique would come from El Grupo Febrero late tonight, claiming responsibility for the deaths of these men.

With the government wiped out, and with the country in total confusion and disarray, General Rodriguez would step forward and offer to form a new government. Ruiz had no doubt that since General Rodriguez was now the number one national hero, the whole country would step into line behind him. Rodriguez's first act as the Head of State would be to declare martial law, which would give him unchecked control. Ruiz, of course, would be the power behind the throne—or in this case, the power behind the dictator.

If anyone objected to Rodriguez's and Ruiz's seizure of power, Ruiz had his stockpiles of weapons to back up their takeover. Ruiz hinted to us darkly that he was in touch with fascistic leaders in the other Western democracies, and that he would do what he could to help them come to power. Ruiz's fantasies extended far beyond ruling Spain. He hoped to have all of Western Europe under his control. It was a mad scheme and one doubted that it would ever work out, and yet . . . look how far Ruiz had come already in achieving his objectives.

Before he left, Ruiz informed us, with his usual sarcasm, that Ramon Lorca had been removed as Head of the Spanish Secret Intelligence. General Rodriguez had publicly accused Lorca of bungling the El Grupo case, and Lorca's duties were being suspended until after an investigation into the matter could be concluded.

Ruiz said it also saddened him to have to tell Pilar and me that we would become, in about twenty minutes, the latest victims of El Grupo Febrero. He would particularly miss his old friend La Condesa Galdos, Ruiz said. On that cheery note he turned and left the room.

I knew that Pilar and I had to figure out a way to get out of here before we became Ruiz's latest pawns—and corpses. But how? I no longer had my luger or my stiletto: Ruiz's men had seen to that. Pilar, however, said that there was a dagger under her dress, held in place by the garter on her right thigh. If I could somehow remove the dagger, we could probably cut the rope that bound our hands. That would be a start.

We stood up, Pilar in back of me, and I moved my bound hands along her body until I felt the metal beneath the silk of her dress. Through the material, I gripped the handle of the dagger in my fingers. I began edging the dagger out of the garter that held it in place, going slowly so I wouldn't jar loose the dagger's sheath and cut Pilar's leg. After a minute or so of concentrated effort, I managed to free the dagger from the garter. I pulled it out from under Pilar's dress by kneeling down. Then I stood up again, and Pilar's hands removed the dagger's sheath.

"Now turn around," I said, "and move your hands up to the dagger." Pilar did as I'd told her to and I began sawing the ropes that bound her hands. Finally, after what seemed an eternity, I felt the rope around her hands giving, and with one last stroke, I severed it. Pilar shook her hands free of the ropes and took the dagger from me. In a few minutes she'd freed the ropes around my hands also.

"Now," I said, "unless they're planning on bombing us in this room, which I doubt, some of Ruiz's men are going to be coming for us soon. Ruiz said twenty mintues and it's probably been about fifteen already. I have a way that I think will get us out of this." I unzipped my pants and untaped Hugo, a tiny bomb, from my upper thigh. "This," I said, holding up the weapon for Pilar to look at, "is a gas bomb. Unlike the gas in Ruiz's chamber, the gas in this little thing is lethal. One whiff and you're gone. Once Ruiz's men come through that door I'm going to toss the bomb. It will kill them within seconds. We're going to have to hold our breaths, and we'll have to run out of here like bats out of hell."

We didn't have long to wait for Ruiz's men. I heard footsteps heading toward the room. The door's lock clicked. Three big bruisers in blue work shirts came through the door.

"Now," I whispered to Pilar. I threw the bomb and it exploded against the chest of the tallest of Ruiz's men. He collapsed, and the other two immediately followed him to the floor. Pilar and I leaped over the bodies and ran out the door into a large bedroom, then through a hall and down a winding staircase.

"Okay," I said at the bottom of the staircase, "you can breathe now." We both gulped greedily for oxygen. We stood in an expensively furnished living room, whose most distinctive features were the bizarrely curved and ornamented walls. I realized that we were in one of the famous Gaudi-designed apartments in downtown Barcelona. A large window looked out across the city, and through it I could see that night had already fallen.

On a table in the middle of the room was some electronic equipment that interested me. It interested me a lot. I recognized the tiny computer, the metal parts and the wires as equipment used to make bombs. Also on the table was a record player and the recording of *Tristan and Isolde* that Pilar and I had heard earlier.

"It looks like Ruiz and his men have been making an audially-controlled bomb," I said to Pilar. "It looks like they've made up something that can be triggered by a certain note in that aria in *Tristan and Isolde*, and most likely the highest note."

"My God, Nick," Pilar cried, "there's a gala performance of *Tristan and Isolde* tonight at the Madrid National Opera House. The King and Queen will be attending. That must be what Ruiz was talking about when he said he'd kill the King tonight. The entire cabinet will be there, too. Ruiz was wearing tails tonight because he was headed to the opera to plant the bomb."

"What time does the opera begin?"

"Eight." I glanced at a clock on the wall. It read 8:30. That meant that it was too late to warn the King and his ministers beforehand. They would have long since left for the opera. I couldn't call Lorca in Madrid and tell him to rush over to the Opera House, because he'd been sacked today. And I didn't want to risk talking to someone else in security about the bomb; Ruiz may have already moved some of his boys in there. The *Lieberstod*, the aria that would trigger the bomb, didn't occur until the third act had almost ended. Pilar and I might be able to make it to Madrid in time to stop the bomb from going off.

"We've got to get there, Pilar. Do you know anyone who can fly us there quick?" She said she did know a man with a helicopter who would probably do it, and she went down the hall to use the telephone. When she returned she nodded her head yes: she'd got the copter.

We commandeered a taxi and arrived at a nearby skyscraper within minutes. On the roof of the building, Pilar's friend had the helicopter's engines already running. We hopped aboard and the plane lifted into the night. As we flew over the peaceful Spanish countryside, Pilar's friend, a large, gruff man in his late forties, handed us two lugers he'd brought us.

"Thought you might need them," he said.

Pilar said simply, "Yes. We will."

Chapter Thirteen

Three quarters of an hour later we stepped out of a taxi and rushed up the broad marble stairs of the National Opera House. In the lobby Pilar smiled at the attendants, who gave us curious glances, marveling I guess, that we would chose to arrive so late for the opera. We may also have looked a little the worse for wear, but at least we were appropriately dressed for the gala, I still had on my tuxedo and Pilar her white silk evening gown of the night before.

"Where are they in the opera?" Pilar asked an attendant as we made our way across the grand promenade.

"Toward the end of the second act, Madame, but you can't go in without tickets."

"I'm La Condesa Galdos," Pilar replied, "and I keep a box here year round. I intend to use my box tonight." We hurried up the stairs to the boxes as the flustered attendant murmured apologies to our backs. Inside Pilar's box we took out opera glasses and tried to scan the gala audience, hoping that we'd be able to spot either Rodriguez or Ruiz. But we couldn't. The lights were turned off, and the

glow the stage cast was not enough to pick out people in the audience. I knew that Rodriguez and
Ruiz had to be here someplace, but we'd have to
wait until the intermission when the second act finished to find out where. I listened to the magisterial
throbbing of Wagner's music and tried to concen-
trate on the mythical figures, bathed in blue lights,
moving across the stage, but I couldn't.

"Does Ruiz keep a box here?" I asked Pilar.

"No, he's usually in Barcelona during the sea-
son."

"Damn. So we'll have to wait and pick him out
of the crowd when the house lights come on."

Finally Tristan and Isolde finished their duet
and the curtain fell. The audience broke into wild
applause, and the singers came out for a curtain
call. Men on the first row tossed up roses to the
woman who had sung Isolde, and when the singers
disappeared behind the curtain, the audience demanded another curtain call. The singers returned
to the front of the stage again.

"Oh, my God!" Pilar exclaimed, clutching at my
arm, "look up, Nick." A white spotlight had come
on and was shining into the gold and crimson
draped box of the Royal Family. There stood the
King and Queen of Spain, smiling and waving
down at the singers, who acknowledged the royal
accolade with extra low bows. With the King and
Queen in the large box were a number of dignitaries, including, I suppose the cabinet members scheduled to attend the gala. And on the
Queen's left was the latest national hero, General
Rodriguez. He was in full-dress uniform, and when
the crowd looked up and saw him, they turned

their attention from the singers and began applauding Rodriguez. As he saluted in acknowledgement, they gave Rodriguez a long sustained ovation, bigger even than the one they'd given to the singers. My heart sank.

As the houselights came on, I noticed Rodriguez talking to the Queen. His body was bent toward her in an apologetic manner. He seemed to be excusing himself, no doubt pleading illness or fatigue due to his recent captivity. The bomb would go off in the next act and Rodriguez, and Ruiz, too, no doubt, would be long gone from the Opera House when the bomb exploded. I had to get at Rodriguez before he left the building. I had to do whatever I could to make him tell me where he and Ruiz had planted the bomb.

The Royal Box was almost exactly opposite Pilar's box in the houseshoe-shaped grand tier. Pilar and I rushed out into the corridor to make our way to the other side of the horseshoe. Unfortunately, we didn't beat the crowd. As soon as the houselights came on, groups of elegantly-dressed men and women had flowed out into the corridor. There was a genteel stampede toward the house bar, which was situated midway on the tier between Pilar's box and that of the Royal Family. We shouldered our way past men in tuxedos and women in their finest silks and chiffons.

The reception that we got from these society people, as we pushed our way past them, wasn't particularly gracious. One man threatened to knock me down when I accidentally jostled his wife, and another man grabbed at Pilar after she'd knocked him out of her way. She gave him a quick clip to the neck and the man let go of her. A shocked murmuring traveled through the crowd. They obviously couldn't figure out why the beautiful lady in the evening gown and the man in the tuxedo were speeding through the *opera* as though they were running a marathon race. Two ushers tried to restrain us, but we shook them off and proceeded on our course.

When we reached the corridor off the Royal Box I checked out the people milling about. Fortunately I towered over the heads of most of the men, and I could see Rodriguez, who stood out in his uniform, in the distance. He was going through an exit door at the end of the corridor.

"Where does that door lead?" I asked Pilar. She said it went to a staircase that led to the upper levels of the Opera House. That probably meant that General Rodriguez was going to make his escape via the roof.

"You follow him," Pilar said, "and I'll try to find the King and Queen and convince them to leave the opera immediately." I elbowed my way past another group of opera-goers and Pilar set off to search for the Royal Family. As I opened the exit door, I discovered that the staircase leading to the building's upper levels was also swarming with people. They were all walking *down* the stairs and it was heavy-going making my way past them.

Then I saw Rodriguez above me on the stairs, also wading through the mass of people. He'd been slowed down by the crowds, and I'd gained on him. He'd apparently made no effort to hurry, not knowing that I was following him.

"*Alto* Rodriguez!" I called up to him. I pulled

the luger Pilar's friend had given me out of my
jacket. Rodriguez turned and searched the crowd
with his eyes.

"*Aquí* Rodriguez!" I said, aiming my gun. When
he saw me, his jaw hardened, then he turned and
fled up the stairs, doubling his pace and frantically
pushing past the people in his way. I couldn't fire
on Rodriguez. I didn't want to risk hitting an innocent bystander and it wouldn't do anyone any good
if I killed Rodriguez before I got the information I
needed out of him. I'd just wanted to halt him with
the gun. Unfortunately, the gun hadn't persuaded
him. The sight of my gun had, however, set up a
wave of shocked whispers and stricken-looking
faces around me. People, no doubt wanting to hu-
mor a crazy man—me—got out of my way. I suppose I should have pulled out the luger before; I
could have got through the crowds easier.

By the time I reached the last turn of the staircase, and the crowd had thinned, I'd again lost
sight of Rodriguez. At the top of the stairs, there
was a door, which had to lead to the roof. I pushed
against it, but it didn't budge. It looked like
Rodriguez had locked it from the outside.

The top landing was fairly narrow, so I didn't
have much room to build up momentum, but I had
to do the best I could and try to break open that
door. I stood as far back from the door as the landing allowed and then rushed forward and heaved
myself against its heavy wooden panels. I felt the
door give slightly outward as a result of my impact,
but it didn't open. I heaved myself against the door
again. Again it stood solid. The third time I put
every ounce of strength I had into crashing against

the door, and this time, as my shoulders hit the wood, I heard the panels splinter as the door began to separate from its hinges. But it still didn't open. The fourth assault did the trick. The door pulled out from its hinges, and I stepped onto the domed roof of the opera house. General Rodriguez was nowhere in sight.

My feet crushed against gravel as I made my way around the elaborate glass and steel dome that stood in the center of the roof. I could hear no voices and no other footsteps on the roof. But when I'd made my way around the south side of the dome, I saw General Rodriguez—and El Conde Ruiz—standing on the southern edge of the roof. They were looking out toward the city, and their backs were toward me. Ruiz had probably been planting the bomb while Rodriguez was with the King and Queen and basking in the glory of the citizens.

Then I saw what the men were looking at in the south. Approaching the roof, from that direction, and already flying low, was a four-seater helicopter. Its lights had been turned out, so as not to attract attention. So that was to be their method of escape! They'd leave behind the bomb, fly off the roof, and when the singer hit that high note and the bomb blew up the Opera House and practically the entire government of Spain, they'd be miles away.

Well, not if I could help it. What I had to do was to shoot down the copter before it landed to whisk them away. If Rodriguez and Ruiz saw that they were going to be stuck at the Opera House, like the rest of us, when the bomb went off, they might break down and tell me where the bomb was planted. But getting down that copter wasn't going to be easy. I knew that I'd have only one shot at it. Once Ruiz and Rodriguez heard my shot, they'd fire on me, and then I'd have my hands full just dodging their bullets and trying to protect myself.

Also, because the pilot of the helicopter had turned off his lights, it was going to be tough making an accurate aim. I'd have to hit the fuel tank in exactly the right place with one shot, or I might as well forget it. I inched myself along the south side of the dome, coming closer to where Rodriguez and Ruiz stood and closer to the helicopter.

The trick was to wait until the helicopter was close enough for me to sight along its fuel tank but not too close to the opera house. If I waited too long, the plane would crash into the building's roof and maybe create as much damage as a bomb itself. Timing was crucial. I moved still closer to the edge of the roof as the helicopter neared the building. Now was the time. I sighted the luger, calculating the exact angle of flight and the speed of the copter in relation to that angle.

I heard the bullet piercing metal and within seconds the helicopter burst into a billowing cloud of orange and yellow flames. Pieces of metal fell from the air, some of them coming within a few feet of the Opera House. I heard the bulk of the plane crash to the ground somewhere nearby, but far enough away to be of no danger to the Opera House. Rodriguez and Ruiz's reaction was not what I'd expected. Perhaps they hadn't realized at first that the crash had been caused by a bullet. They stood as still as statues, apparently mesmerized by the sight of the destruction of their means of excape. Their backs were still toward me.

"Hands above your heads," I yelled at them.
"You're covered." Both men jumped at the sound
of my voice. I thought for a second that Rodriguez
was actually going to pitch off the roof. But they
put their hands where I wanted them to.

"Now turn around." The faces they turned to
me were glowering with rage and disappointment.

"You goddamned fool, Carter," Rodriguez
screamed hysterically at me, "now you'll kill us
all."

"Not if you tell me where the bomb is. The third
act of the opera has already begun, and there's not
much time left before it goes off, is there?"

"It's in an empty box on tier one," Rodriguez
began nervously.

"Shut up, you bastard," Ruiz screamed, trying
to stop Rodriguez.

But General Rodriguez was not a brave man.
"It's in box seventeen-right," he said.

Ruiz shouted a string of curses at Rodriguiz, his
voice rising in fury.

"You stupid bastard!" he yelled. "You swine!
You try to ruin the plan I've been working on
for years, you try to prevent me from ruling this
country!" He'd become completely irrational.
Rodriguez stood there dumbstruck by Ruiz's in-
vective, and before I realized what was happening,
Ruiz had pulled out a pistol and fired at Rodriguiz.
I shot the gun out of Ruiz's hand before he had
time to vent his rage anymore, but his first shot had
hit Rodriguez, whose body crumpled to the gravel.
Blood seeped through the front of his uniform and
his breath was coming in short gasps.

Ruiz took off in a run across the roof. I fired at him, but he managed to dodge my first bullet. By the time I fired a second time, he'd disappeared around the glass dome. I started after him, and I heard an exchange of gunshots ring out. Glass shattered as a bullet hit one of the panes of the dome. Ruiz must have had a second gun, but who was he firing at?

"Nick!" It was Pilar's voice.

"Over here!" She came rushing around the dome, gun in hand. She stopped when she saw General Rodriguez lying there.

"Thank God, Nick. I thought you were dead when I saw Ruiz running across the roof just as I came up."

"Are you all right?"

"I'm fine. Did you find out where the bomb is?"

"Yes."

"Then you better get down there quick. I couldn't get past the security guards to the King and Queen. Apparently Lorca wasn't the only one that Rodriguez has been spreading tales about. No one would listen to me."

"Rodriguez won't be spreading tales any more," I said, looking down at the body that was now a corpse. "Did you see which way Ruiz headed?"

"Yeah, there's another exit from the roof, which leads backstage. It looked like that's where he was going."

"Okay," I said to Pilar. "You try to find him and I'll go after the bomb. Rodriguez said it was in one of the boxes."

I rushed to the roof exit and made my way down the stairs three at a time. As I reached the top tier,

I could hear the dramatic crescendo of the *Lieberstod*, the twenty-minute aria that Isolde sings about the death of Tristan. The music had already begun to build towards its climax, which meant that I only had a short time, maybe five minutes at most, to find the bomb and get it out of the building. When Isolde hit her high note, which was the peak of the aria, the musically-triggered bomb would explode.

After what seemed like the largest number of steps I'd ever descended, I reached the grand tier. I ran along the corridor following the numbers of the boxes until I came to number seventeen-right. A startled usher, a long-faced man, with thinning hair and thick glasses, jumped out of the chair where he was resting as I passed him.

"Hey," he yelled after me.

He was on my heels when I entered the box that Rodriguez had specified.

"Sir," the usher said, "this is a private box, you can't just go in here." I'd already begun searching the deserted box. I turned over one plush-covered Louis XIV chair after another, checking underneath them for the bomb.

"Sir," said the usher, as he watched me hurl around the furniture, "you can't do this. Do you know the property you're handling is owned by the State? Stop that. This is an outrage." Ignoring him, I ripped back the heavy velvet drapes which swathed the sides of the box. Nothing was behind them except walls in need of a paint job.

"Sir . . . " the usher began again, his voice getting more and more indignant. He was beginning to get on my nerves. I pulled out the luger and waved it in his direction. His face turned white, and he muttered something about calling security as he backed out of the room. I moved to the edge of the box and checked under the ornate gold railing. Nothing was there except dust and some hardened wads of chewing gum. I guess even society folks have their bad habits. Leaning over the railing, I saw that the box I was in was only two boxes down from the King's. Ruiz certainly wasn't taking any chances in killing the man he so hated. Even if, by some miracle, the bomb didn't destroy everyone in the opera house when it went off, if sure as hell was going to get the King and his ministers.

Isolde's lament for Tristan was becoming louder and more intense. It seemed very close to its climax. Where the hell could a bomb be in an opera box other than under the chairs or railing or behind the drapes? It crossed my mind then to try to stop the opera. I'd yell down to the singer to stop her aria, and I'd even threaten her with my luger if I had to. If she wouldn't stop, I'd have to shoot her. I didn't like the idea, but politically, and even statistically, it seemed the only action possible. One innocent death in exchange for hundreds, perhaps thousands of deaths, and the destruction of the entire Spanish government and its head.

I pulled out my luger. Then I saw an ornate marble column to the side of the box. Except it was peculiar; it didn't go completely to the top of the ceiling, it missed by several inches. Up close I could see that it wasn't real marble at all, but wood painted to look like marble. With one ferocious karate kick I split the wood near the column's base. Another kick made a large opening in the wood. I reached my hand down into the column. My fingers touched something solid, covered with paper. I worked the package up to the opening I'd made and pulled it out. I'd found the bomb all right: a small cube wrapped in brown paper.

But I was afraid I might have found the package too late. The music was now a pounding swell of orchestration and the singer's notes were already piercing: the human voice doesn't stretch many notes higher.

Package in hand, I rushed out of the box. Right into the arms of two opera Security Guards. The long-faced usher stood beside them, a smug look on his pasty features. "He's the one," the usher said, and the guards grabbed my arms.

"I've got a bomb in this package!" I shouted above the now deafening music. "If you fellows don't let me go immediately, we're all going to be blown to hell! It's the work of El Grupo Febrero, and it's meant to kill the King!" I guess the guards heard me above the music and I guess they believed me too. Maybe it was because I'd used the magic code word: El Grupo Febrero. They took their hands off my arms. The usher heard me too. He cowered against the wall. His face was a mixture of terror and sheepishness.

I rushed to the closest window in sight. It was an elaborately mullioned affair, and I sent the bomb crashing through its glass panes just seconds before Isolde hit her death-signaling note. The package sailed through the air and landed in the grass of a small park next to the Opera House, safely out of audial range. I'd made it. And the soprano had made her high note.

Now I had to find Ruiz and Pilar. But the Opera Security guards had come up to me and looked ready to pounce on me once again.

"I'm from Spanish Intelligence," I said tersely, hoping that would keep their paws off me.

"Are you here with General Rodriguez?" one of them asked, eyeing me suspiciously.

"General Rodriguez is up on the roof," I said. "He's dead." Before they had time to compose their faces and close their open mouths, I headed off down the corridor.

Backstage, on the stage's left wing, I found a group of performers and stagehands gathered around a figure lying on the floor. As I came closer, I noticed the hem of a white satin dress. The person lying there was Pilar! My heart leapt up into my throat as I pushed my way through the crowd. The skirt of Pilar's white dress was streaked with blood. Her face was pale and her eyes were fighting back tears, but she was alive. The house doctor was beside her. I knelt down and took her hand.

"Pilar, what happened?"

"It's nothing, Nick," she said, although it was obvious she was in pain. "Ruiz shot me in the thigh as I was chasing him down the stairs from the roof. I followed him as far as I could, but eventually it became too hard, my leg just gave out. I couldn't keep up with him any more. But it's only a surface wound. I'll be okay." The doctor beside her nodded his head to reassure me.

"Which way did he go, Pilar?"

"Up that way," she said, pointing to a set of narrow iron stairs to our right. A bystander volunteered the information that the stairs led up to the backdrop area, which was above and behind the opera's stage. Once someone was up there, the only way to get back down was to return down these stairs. So it looked like we had Ruiz trapped. I told the stage manager to post several security guards at the foot of the stairs. If anything happened to me, they were to shoot Ruiz as he came down.

"Nick," Pilar said. "Ruiz is unarmed. I shot his gun out of his hand as he went up those stairs."

"Good," I said. "That means we can fight man to man." I dropped my gun to the floor and bent to kiss Pilar.

Then I began my climb up the metal staircase.

This was it: either I was going to kill El Conde Ruiz now, or he'd have to kill me. Rodriguez was already gone, and with Ruiz dead, El Grupo Febrero would be out of operation. Their men were hired criminals and disenchanted psychopaths. Leaderless and without Ruiz's money and resources, they would flounder.

When I reached the top of the staircase, I found myself in an enormous, three-sided room. The room had no fourth wall; instead there was a steel railing where the room's wooden floor abruptly ended. Beyond the railing you could see the lighting banks and the catwalks above the stage. Large, thick ropes, used to lower scenery, hung just on the other side of the railing. The only illumination up here was provided by the stage lights in the distance. The last scene of *Tristan and Isolde* is played in low blue light. Up here the blue was even dimmer, and the ropes beside the railing cast eerie shadows across the room's floor.

Enormous panels, backdrops for various operas, leaned against the walls. Large, free-standing structures that on stage would represent country inns and taverns and caves were scattered about the room. Ruiz could be behind any of them. Smaller props lay about, here and there: the Lady of the Camillia's fan. Othello's dagger, the horned headdresses of the Valkyrie. I moved slowly to the center of the room, keeping my eyes on the shadowed structures around me. I stood beside the front wall of a Renasssance Palace fashioned out of wooden beams and papier-mache. From the darkness at the end of the room, I heard some movement. I turned and peered in that direction, and slowly I made my way toward the area I'd heard the noise come from. Then, there was a flurry of movement and suddenly I saw one of the enormous wood and canvas backdrops come crashing down toward my head. I turned and fled away from the backdrop, but its wooden edge hit my shoulders and the back of my neck. I staggered forward from the tremendous force of the backdrop's weight, and I heard it crash to the floor at my heels. Had it fallen directly on top of me, I would have been dead.

Turning back around, I saw Ruiz running toward me from the darkness. Stretched out before him was a long spear, like the ones the servants carry in *Aida*. The spear's sharp-pointed tip was aimed at my chest. I jumped in time to miss its thrust. Ruiz quickly turned around and came at me again, yelling, "I'll kill you yet Carter."

But I stepped aside just as the weapon neared my head, and its tip sunk into the papier-mache wall of the palace beside me. As Ruiz tried to pull the spear out of the fake building, I came on him from behind and landed a sharp blow against his solar plexus that left him gasping. I picked him up and threw him over my head. He landed on his back on the hard wooden floor. He cried out in pain, but he immediately scrambled back up to his feet.

We now stood face to face in the center of the room. "You've done your best to destroy my plans," Ruiz said. "but now I'm going to destroy you. I'll triumph in spite of you. You forget that I still have nuclear weapons at my disposal, once I get out of here." I hadn't forgotten, and that's why I was up here, to keep Ruiz from ever leaving this building. To destroy the madman once and for all. I went after him. I grabbed him around the waist, and, putting my foot behind his heel, I wrestled him to the floor. We rolled around in the dust for awhile, and finally I managed to get him underneath me.

I pummeled his handsome face with my fist again and again. I pummeled him for Maria and for Pedro and for the men he'd held captive. I pummeled him for his kidnap victims and for the people who had died as a result of his bombs. His nose broke beneath the force of my blows and blood oozed out of his cut-up mouth. But then he got his hands between my legs and squeezed my balls with such force that I winced. His other fist came up suddenly and collided against my jaw with such impact that I fell backwards.

Ruiz jumped up and ran toward me. He jumped, with the force of his entire body, on top of my rib cage. I felt a bone or two crack and the air rushed out of my lungs. Ruiz's heavy military boots kicked out at my face. I felt the taste of blood in my mouth where one of his kicks had landed. Taking advantage of my temporarily breathless condition, Ruiz came down on top of me, straddling me and pinioning my arms to my side with his heavily muscled legs. Then he placed his hands around my neck and began squeezing. Above me, Ruiz's mouth opened in a diabolical grin. His blood-drenched face, with its now broken nose, was no longer handsome. It had become a distorted devil's mask. A hysterical cackle rose from Ruiz's throat as he pressed his hands against my throat, harder and harder. I felt the blood rush to my head and my breaths becoming shorter and shorter.

I struggled, trying to free my arms from the vise of Ruiz's thighs. Finally I managed to slide my left arm out from under him. I put all the strength I could muster into my fist and struck out at him. My blow landed just below his right rib cage. Ruiz reeled slightly backwards, and the pressure against my neck decreased. I knew that this slight braking of his strength was the last chance I'd have to get away from him. I heaved myself up and strained with all my strength against Ruiz's body. His muscles gave way before mine and eventually I freed my neck from his hands and threw him off of me. Ruiz rose from the floor as I lay panting, spent from the struggle. Catching my breath I pulled myself to a standing position and advanced on Ruiz.

Then unexpectedly Ruiz turned and ran toward the railing above the opera stage. He climbed over the railing, and for a second I thought he was going to jump. Instead he reached out and grabbed one of the heavy ropes hanging nearby. I ran after him, but just as I reached the railing, Ruiz, clinging to the rope, propelled himself away from my grasp. He sailed out across the area directly above the opera's stage. He managed to land on a narrow catwalk above the center of the stage. After he'd secured his footing, he let go of the rope. From the catwalk he looked back at me, grinning triumphantly. Ruiz glanced to his right, and it was then that I realized that the catwalk had to lead off to the right wing, and that there would be a ladder there to the ground. He might escape after all. I considered grabbing a rope and propelling myself to the catwalk. But then I thought of something else.

I ran back to the center of the scenery room and grabbed Othello's gold dagger. Back at the railing, I saw Ruiz cautiously making his way across the narrow catwalk. I yelled at him, and he turned toward me, still smiling victoriously.

The smile did not have time to fade before the gold dagger sunk straight into Ruiz's evil heart. Blood spurted from his chest and his body swayed backwards and plunged to the stage far below. The final note of the opera sounded as I looked down. The real corpse lay among all the opera's fake corpses, center stage. And then the curtain fell.

NICK CARTER

"Nick Carter out-Bonds James Bond."
—<u>Buffalo Evening News</u>

Exciting, international espionage adventure with Nick Carter, Killmaster N3 of AXE, the super-secret agency!

☐ **THE ULTIMATE CODE**   84308-5 $1.50
Nick Carter delivers a decoding machine to Athens—and finds himself in a CIA trap.

☐ **BEIRUT INCIDENT**   05378-5 $1.50
Killmaster infiltrates the Mafia to stop a new breed of underworld killer.

☐ **THE NIGHT OF THE AVENGER**   57496-3 $1.50
From Calcutta, to Peking, to Moscow, to Washington, AXE must prevent total war.

☐ **THE SIGN OF THE COBRA**   76346-4 $1.50
A bizarre religious cult plus a terrifying discovery join forces against N3.

☐ **THE GREEN WOLF CONNECTION**   30328-5 $1.50
Middle-eastern oil is the name of the game, and the sheiks were masters of terror.

Available wherever paperbacks are sold or use this coupon.

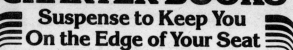

CHARTER BOOKS
Opens the Door to A World of Mystery

Edgar Award Winner Donald E. Westlake
King of the Caper

WHO STOLE SASSI MANOON?   88592-6   **$1.95**
Poor Sassi's been kidnapped at the film festival — and it's the most fun she's had in years.

THE FUGITIVE PIGEON   25800-X   **$1.95**
Charlie Poole had it made — until his Uncle's mob associates decided Charlie was a stool pigeon. See Charlie fly!

THE BUSYBODY   68555-5   **$1.95**
First they gave Brody a classic gangland funeral. Then they went to dig him up. The empty coffin didn't do much to make anyone feel secure.

The Mitch Tobin Mysteries
by Tucker Coe

KINDS OF LOVE, KINDS OF **DEATH**	44467-9	**$1.95**
THE WAX APPLE	87397-9	**$1.95**
A JADE IN ARIES	38075-1	**$1.95**
DON'T LIE TO ME	15835-8	**$1.95**
